BROKEN

Also by James E. Ferrell

Cross-Pull
Doing Time in Texas – The Series
Book 1: *Always Have a Plan*
Book 2: *For Love of Money*
Book 3: *Every Road Leads to Huntsville*
Cross-Pull (Second Edition)
Winter Crossing
Broken
Book 1: Broken Peace
Book 2: Broken Pieces
Book 3: Broken Reckoning

Books Soon to Come by James E. Ferrell
Class of 64

CONTACT US:
Grey Ghost Publisher
19431 Highway 30 #36
Shiro, TX 77876
or
greyghostpublisher2@gmail.com
On Facebook **@JamesEFerrell123**
https://greyghost23.us2.authorhomepage.com

BROKEN

Book 1: Broken Peace

Book 2: Broken Pieces

Book 3: Broken Reckoning

Written by James E. Ferrell

Co-written & edited by Kathryn H. Clair

Published by
Grey Ghost Publisher
19431 Highway 30 #36
Shiro, Texas 77876

Ferrell & Clair

Co-author: Kathryn H. Clair
Published by:
Grey Ghost Publisher, 19431 Highway 30 #36, Shiro, Texas 77876
Printed in the United States of America by Amazon
This book is printed on acid-free paper.

Publisher's Cataloging-in-Publication data
Names: Ferrell, James E., author. | Clair, Kathryn H., author.
Title: Broken , book 3: broken reckoning / written by James E. Ferrell; co-written and edited by Kathryn H. Clair.
Description: Shiro, TX: Grey Ghost Publisher, 2023.
Identifiers: LCCN: 2023908877 | ISBN 978-1-950763-31-3 (hardcover) | 978-1-950763-30-6 (paperback) | 978-1-950763-32-0 (ebook)
Subjects: LCSH United States--Territorial expansion--Fiction. | Texas--History--19th century--Fiction. | West (U.S.)--History--19th century--Fiction. | Indians of North America--Fiction. | Western fiction. | Historical fiction. | Christian fiction. | FICTION / Christian / Western | FICTION / Christian / Romance | FICTION / Historical / Civil War | FICTION / Women
Classification: LCC PS3606.E77 B76 2023 | DDC 813.6--dc23

Acknowledgment

This book is dedicated to rural America that I knew as a youth and a people living close to the land.

The Author's Pen

The battle is always uphill. One never knows from day today what tomorrow will bring. Our lives are like a puzzle with many different shaped pieces. We seem to be able to put the most obvious pieces into the puzzle with ease when we are very young. You know, the corner pieces! As time goes by, the pieces get harder to figure out and we try to put the square peg in the round hole, so to speak. As the last ones are staring us in the face, we look and place the puzzle pieces where they belong. Aww, but that last puzzle piece is the sweetest. That is the one God puts in for us.

It is Sunday afternoon under a very overcast sky. The wind is kicking up, and the back pasture is rich and green with good grass for my cows. Rain is the main need for farmers and ranchers who depend on good grass. Birds are singing. Hummingbirds are racing from feeder to feeder, pulling the rich nectar from the red bottles. I say this to let you know that all seems well in the animal world. I know that is not so with mankind. All the people I know experience brokenness. Hearts and minds are broken. My pastor has leukemia and just went through back surgery. His sweet wife had brain cancer. He lost her before I finished this book. The Bible says God makes us one flesh with our spouse, so his lot is worse than I can imagine. They have spent their lives doing the Lord's work together. Serving and ultimately laying to rest the members of the little flock God has entrusted to them.

My friend Joan, who in the past greeted me with a smile at the local lumber yard, has been fighting cancer for twelve years. Like me, she wakes each morning thanking God for another day. My younger brother is dealing with cancer. Here I sit looking at a steady rain and am at peace, except…I am broken. I am dealing with stage four bone cancer. I have made a year with this my second round of cancer. Many more of those I love dearly are fighting something in their lives that have broken their hearts, adding daily grief and pain to their world.

I know how life is, and God has been very good to me. So, as I sit here and consider my lot, I think **Broken** is a good name, a very good name, for this trilogy. Now if my sweet editor and co-author, as well as our Beta readers, can smooth out all the bumps, the books should be ready for our readers' consumption. God Bless all that read them.

I dedicate this book **Broken** to my brother Thomas (Tom) *who is fighting the good fight* and all that are walking the long dark valley, knowing that somewhere ahead, the valley ends.

James E. Ferrell

Previews

Ordinarily, previews of the books are written for each individual book, even in a trilogy. However, this year has been a tough one for us. Things started to be processed finally, and before we knew it, all three books of the trilogy were finished! Our Beta Readers received all three books at one time and therefore were able to preview them as a whole. Hence, the same preview will be printed in each book of **Broken**

Broken...what a trilogy for the person who is interested in the Old West. The Christian values of the born again and the Hope of Redemption! James Ferrell has written a sweeping trilogy of the West and interfaced it well with the values of life as well as the values of the Christian life. The books are like grabbing a bad bull by the tail, how do you let go?

I could not! Almost at once I became a settler, a survivor, a desperate fugitive, and several other personas as I was pulled into the tragedies and victories of the various characters in his broad story of life and death from the towns, plains, rivers, and mountains of the character's experiences.

To anyone who enjoys a mixture of twists and turns and subplots galore, welcome to a shoot 'em up full fisted read!

To be in any sense critical, my only problem is tracking the number of characters. This is James Ferrell at his best though, mixing and meandering storylines of a plethora of people into a mega story or stories of their lives and faults and successes of life by sharing the impact and power of how Christ can and does affect the lives of ordinary and extraordinary people!

Way to go James!

Robert Nichols, II
Pastor, Cook Springs Baptist
Church

Join James Ferrell as he takes a group of brave travelers westward while they dream of a new life. On the way, they encounter sickness, savage Indians, and death. Their faith in God never wavers as they reach their new homes in the Hill Country of Texas and the new lives of which they dreamed.

Nita M.

Broken is a rootin', tootin', western adventure trilogy of life in the new West spun up by a fine pair of storytellers, James Ferrell and Kathy Clair. You will not want to quit turning the pages. Get all three of these books lined up so you do not have to stop until the end.

It has everything! The characters are filled with the despair of broken families caused by the hardships and the renewal of faith as they struggle through putting their lives back together. This is a collection of rousing action and adventures during the development of the western parts of our country in the mid-1800s. Tales of cowboys and Indians, settlers, mountain men, and returning civil war veterans as they all moved West with most seeking new, prosperous, and happy lives while the Indians, owlhoots and outlaws with their dastardly deeds seek them out as prey. The West was rough country with murderous Indian and Comancheros raids, attacks on wagon trains, settlers, fledgling communities, and the kidnapping and brutalization of survivors. This tough new breed of American pioneers struggled mightily to bring civilization to this rough land.

They brought their hopes and dreams of a new life and most importantly, the "Faith of Our Fathers" to guide and see them through their struggles and hardship in the new territory. They trusted that this faith would guide them through those things beyond their control in the trials ahead of them. All these stories and characters are skillfully intertwined throughout the series and fold together along the way bringing the resolution from their choices in their lives and how the results of their choices have affected others. Characters are pressured by circumstance and wander from decency and goodness to lives of crime and despotism. Surprises abound as these people, both good and bad, discover what decency lives within even the worst of them and that their eternal life can be assured.

James and Kathy also show throughout **Broken** that those that were exposed to the teachings of the Bible at any time during their lives from childhood forward even though they might have grown to be thoroughly despicable still carried the flicker of that flame of Christianity. It returns to burn brighter than ever once the breath of the God brings it back to life. These are stories of human failings, sorrow and heartache, and the joy of the reunification of families, and redemption sprinkled with a delightful humor throughout that will warm your heart. I cannot wait for the next ones!

J. Stevens

Broken is a trilogy of compelling stories of war, life on the trail and how it affected the lives of those who endured and survived. It warmed my heart to see the lasting friendships that were made and their dependence on each other. Each book left me wanting to read more.

Lynda B.

Table of Contents

Also by James E. Ferrell.. ii

Acknowledgment v

The Author's Pen vi

Previews.. viii

Table of Contents.. xii

List of Series Main Characters in Alphabetical Order xiii

Introduction.. xvi

C01 - Bob 1

C02 - A Personal Matter 12

C03 - Miller's Revelation 28

C04 - Broken Reckoning... 38

C05 - Facing Death Straight On 48

C06 - Provisions Offered.. 60

C07 – Uncertain Future 69

C08 - The Wages of Sin.. 80

C09 – Memories 85

C10 - Broken Past... 91

C11 - The Second Fiddle Man 109

C12 - High Places.. 128

C13 - Visions in Clay 139

C14 - The Grief of Sin and the Marvel of Grace 147

C15 - The Longworth Episode... 153

C16 - A Cup of Tremble 163

C17 - Birds of a Feather 183

C18 - Reflections... 189

C19 – The Hills of Home 197

C20 - A Dark Wind Blows.. 205

C21 – Hard Explanations 219

C22 – Old Memories 232

C23 – Broken Reasoning 242

C24 – Well-Planned Evil... 263

C25 – Where Do We Start? 274

C26 - A Disappearing Act 281

C27 – The Piece That Brings Peace 283

A Cowboy's Prayer in a Broken World 290

List of Series Main Characters in Alphabetical Order

Abe Styles – Rancher, on Nolan Tolivar's wagon train

Abel Blackburn – a 17-year-old young man who took over a cattle drive when his father died suddenly

Alison Smith – Friend of Joe Bess / part of the Hill Country Gang

Bald Jo Kline / Black Hawk / Henry Jackson / Don Jo Verde – young Black slave, sold to Mexican Don / traded to Apache tribe / chief of the Blackfoot of the Apache / feared by all

Ben Turner – Physician / preacher / friend to the Hill Country Gang

Bo Connors – Friend of Joe Bess / part of the Hill Country Gang / parents from Ireland

Calvin Ben Lacy – Son of Samantha and Bald Jo Kline / raised by Horace and Samantha

Christian Murdock – son of Jason Murdock and White Cloud

Dotty Baker – Ellen's daughter / on Nolan Tolivar's wagon train

Erlinda McAllen – female physician caring for the people of Paso Verde, Mexico

Drovers: worked for Abel Blackburn
JD
Jones
Miller
Red

Ed Bellows – Frank Bellows' son / crook

Elizabeth Masters – Wife of Jonathan / accompanying Jonathan to the West / on Captain Billy Snow's wagon train

Francis Littlefield – ex-Comanchero / Paso Verde Blacksmith and preacher

Frank Bellows – The Golden Rose Saloon owner and crook

Hank Lightfoot – Christian Comanche / Professor / appointed Chief of the Bidai Indians / father was a Comanche Indian

Horace Lacy – Physician / husband of Samantha / Raised Calvin as his son

Indian Chiefs
>
> Broken Knife
> Buffalo Rump
> Dark Cloud
> Ragin Bull
> Thunder Cloud

Isaac Bell – Black man sold to a Don in Mexico and subsequently traded by Comancheros to the Apache after Don was murdered

Isabella McAllen – daughter of Dr. Erlinda McAllen and Bald Jo Kline

Jason Murdock – settler in Missouri / cousin to Samantha Lacy

Jasper Bess – Ex-con on Nolan's wagon train

Jemima Long – Abel's girlfriend

Jericho Dawson – Trapper

Jessica Blackburn – Stony's wife

Joe Bess / Riley – son of Jasper and Dotty Bess

Jonathan Masters – Professor in Rhode Island / traveling on Captain Billy Snow's wagon train / husband to Elizabeth Masters

June Walsh – Saloon manager for Bellows

Lone Eagle – father of White Cloud / grandfather of Christian Murdock and Running Deer

Longworth – a crook who tried to steal Abel's cattle

Major Jesse Killeen – Union Officer assigned to the Texas Hill Country region

Modena – Trail hand / fired by Abel

Nolan Tolivar – Wagon Master

Pate Ledbetter – Crook / murderer

Patrick Murphy – Uncle of William Murphy

Pete Cooper – Friend of Ben Turner and the Hill Country Gang

Professor Lightfoot – Comanche Indian / father of Hank / educated in the East / La Fuego, TX, schoolteacher

Reddy Bell – Son of Isaac Bell / half Black-half Apache / part of the Hill Country Gang / friend to Joe Bess

Running Deer – daughter of Jason Murdock and White Cloud

Samantha Lacy – wife of Horace / taken by Bald Jo Kline in Billy Snow wagon train massacre

Sarah Walsh – younger sister of June Walsh

Stony Blackburn – Trail Boss / father of Abel / died on the cattle drive

Tindal Sloan – Texas Ranger
Trappers:
       Buster Franks
       Frank Pepper
       Pike Smithers

White Cloud – Indian maiden who married Jason Murdock

William Murphy – young boy taken by Osage Indians when his family was massacred

Workers for Don Jo Verde:
       Araña (Spider)
       Mateo
       Pablo

Introduction

Each day we spend in this life has a profound influence on souls around us. Book three is the collection of souls on the highway of life.

One of the main characters, Bald Jo Kline (aka Black Hawk and Don Jo Verde, to mention only a few of the aliases he had), was born in freedom in Africa, sold into slavery in America, sold to a don in Mexico, traded for whisky to the Apache, and finally became a feared leader in the Indian nation. Jo found himself in the fight of his life. Does he live or die?

Dr. Erlinda McAllen, a victim of Black Hawk's raids on her grandfather's land. 13 years later, she is faced with her hatred for him and all Indians because of the atrocities dealt to her. However, how does a savage change his life? How did he change her life?

Miller was a drover who found himself in several situations linked together that took him from one close call to another. Finally, on a rain-soaked night, he gets it and life changes for him. His only companion to share his joy is old Bob. A mutt that was at best worthless, a flea-bitten hound of no value. Just an animal to share a meal.

William Murphy found himself in the worst possible situation. He was too young to stand against the evil wind that blew in his life. He found himself alone in a world where no one who would have cared knew he was still alive.

Jericho Dawson wandered the wilderness. He knew the wilderness was like a lovely woman. One minute she loved you and the next you were running for your life. Generally stripped of all you valued.

Most of the characters of the first two books are trudging through their lives in book three, as well as other books this author has written. They reached a point when they had done all they could do, so they took a stand hoping for the best. Looking back in retrospect along their highway of life, they realized their lives held little or no significance. In Book Three, each character had their moments of great remorse, despair, and for some, great hope. In this boken world, there are just too many people that do not realize they are standing close to the edge. They know of no one who can fix their brokenness.

I hope you enjoy **Broken**. Many characters you read about in my other books are here in **Broken**. It is a work of the heart, and I include it in my unspoken prayers from start to finish. God Bless all who read Kathy's and my novel called **Broken**.

Ferrell & Clair

BROKEN

Book 1: Broken Peace

Book 2: Broken Pieces

Book 3: Broken Reckoning

Ferrell & Clair

C01 - Bob

Miller and Jones left long before sunrise. They sat on their horses before the first shadows appeared, glaring into the shadowy morning. They lay awake all night, wondering if their friend was dead or alive. They could wait no longer. If JD was alive, they wanted to ensure that he stayed that way. "We are close to where the herd was when we started running them. According to the hair on the back of my neck, I'd say we are not alone," Jones whispered.

A mist-thickened, heavy fog settled across the prairie, making the cowboys cold and wet. In the darkness, an undistinguishable sound caused them to draw their rifles. Pulling up, they sat on their horses; only the occasional creak of leather broke the silence. A horse whinnied out in the fog.

"That sounds like JD's horse. He must have caught the scent of our horses," Miller said. Jones' horse whinnied, and suddenly the sound of a running horse echoed across the prairie as JD's horse, Apache, raced up to their familiar horses.

"Wooooo boy," Jones whispered as the horse came close to him. The horse shied, but the familiar voice had a settling effect on Apache, and he circled to stop alongside the horse Jones rode.

"We have JD's horse, and there's blood on the saddle," Miller said. Movement in the tall grass sent Miller and Jones to the ground. Neither man said anything but kept their rifles ready. Their horses stood over them, and JD's horse Apache snorted and shied off a few steps. "That horse is one smart critter. I rather have him around than my cow dog!"

"Which reminds me," Miller whispered, "Where is that blasted dog of yorn?"

"When we stampeded the herd, Bob up and ran away. The last I heard him bark, he was just off to our right," Jones whispered.

Apache's head went up, and Miller and Jones eased the hammers back on their rifle. Suddenly Apache bolted and ran into the foggy morning. Two warriors came out of the grass. They had crawled within a few yards of the two before rising from the prairie grass. One went down, hit by both of their bullets before the other drove a spear into Jones' side. Miller rolled over onto his knees and shot him at point-blank range. Crawling around in the deep grass, Miller checked to see how badly Jones was hurt. The spear had Jones' shirt pinned to the ground and a small cut down his side.

"Miller," Jones whispered as he added shells to his rifle. "You shot the wrong Injun, and the one you were supposed to shoot—done speared me!"

"Sorry, I thought he was yorn'— We'll talk about that later. For now, pay attention, won't you?" Miller said.

"That crazy hoss of JD's done saved our bacon," Jones said in a nervous whisper.

"He ain't here to do it again, so shut up and be watchful!" Miller stated emphatically.

The morning light started to cast shadows through the fog. Rifle shots echoed across the prairie, and Miller's horse buckled and fell dead. Jones heard the slugs hit and rolled away from Miller's big horse to keep from being crushed.

"Now, we have something to hide behind," Jones whispered as he tried to bandage his side with a sleeve he tore from his shirt.

"Reb—was the best cow hoss I ever owned," Miller whispered.

"I never heard you say a good thing about this hoss until he dropped dead. Now, suddenly, he's the best hoss you ever owned. Daylight is coming, and we are in the middle of an open prairie hiding behind a dead horse. This ain't good, Miller—this ain't good at all," Jones said.

Across the prairie, a firefight broke out and lasted only a few seconds. They breathed shallowly, fearing they might give their position away. Jones retrieved his saddlebags from his mount. "Miller, my horse has also been shot," Jones said. Grumbling to himself, he stripped the saddle and sent him out across the prairie at a run, not wanting the next shot to kill his horse. "Well, now it looks like we are both afoot," Jones said.

"That sounded like a repeater. Now, who do you suppose that is? I thought we were the only people on this blasted prairie aside from the Indians," Miller said.

"It was a repeater rifle for sure. It must be JD putting up a fight. Let's make our way over there and take a closer look," Jones said.

"I'm getting kind of fond of this big hoss of yours. He is about the only cover on this prairie," Jones said.

"Give him a few hours, and you will lose any attachment you might have. Let's move!" Getting up cautiously, Miller retrieved his saddle and tack from the dead horse. Every sound they made seemed magnified on the open prairie. A few scattered cedar bushes added to their caution. They were expecting to see warriors rush upon them at any time.

"We are about where the drag would have been when we started the stampede last night," Jones whispered.

In the distance, Apache, JD's horse, pranced across the prairie, whinnying, his head high. "Jones, look, JD's hoss is looking for him. We will just follow along after him," Miller said. The horse moved for a few hundred yards before stopping short of a triangle of boulders that outcropped from the center of the prairie. Three dead braves lay near each other. "Three of them all shot dead. They were after someone in those rocks over there," Miller said. Apache circled the boulders and then moved in behind them.

"JD, if you are alive, don't you be a-shootin'! It's me and Miller," Jones called out as they approached the rock formation.

"I know Miller, but who is me?" JD called back.

"He's all right. Still got his sense of humor," Jones said.

"What took you so long?" a familiar voice from behind the rocks asked.

A bloody-headed JD rose weakly from the boulders and patted Apache's neck. Easing himself down on a boulder, he rubbed his bloodshot eyes. "They found me just before daylight. That was the longest night of my life. If it hadn't been for them Injun kids, yours truly would have been scalped for sure. You boys store your saddles in these rocks," JD said.

Jones and Miller gave each other a questioning look and scanned the prairie. Miller asked, "Pardon me for asking, JD, but who are you talking about?"

With Miller's help, JD stood on wobbly legs. He was a sight; blood had hardened, making a patch of reddish-brown twisted hair on his head that covered his left ear. His left arm had been grazed, and blood had run down his arm into his glove. "My—my feller, you are a sight—looks like you've had yourself a fun night. Can you elaborate on those Injun kids?" Miller asked.

"Well—I—I—there was a couple of young Injuns—a boy and girl what dragged me in behind these rocks. Actually, they were White children. They told me to be quiet because warriors were out in the tall grass looking for me," JD explained.

"Now it's White children? Miller, I'm a-thinkin'—JD's head wound is a lot worse than it looks," Jones said.

"You're thinking right, Jones, but I'm more concerned about the warriors out in this tall grass for now. We need to be a-movin'. Help me get JD on his horse, and we will tie him on. The way I see it, you can ride double on JD's horse and hold him in place. I'll walk behind. If anything happens, hightail it for camp," Miller said.

"Miller, I'm not leaving you afoot out here. We will stay together. JD, do we need to tie you to your saddle?" Jones said.

"I can hang on; just get me to the camp. This prairie is not a place I'm fond of," JD said.

The sound of a running horse got their attention. "We got company coming! Looks like the boss! It's a good thing he's the boss because he doesn't know how to take orders. He was supposed to stay with the herd. We are still a couple of horses short on this ride," Miller said.

"You boys ran off and left me this morning. Don't worry. I left Red with the herd, and he has plenty of company. Miller, your horse, is lying back there dead. I didn't bring any spare mounts," Abel said.

"The boss says he left Red in charge of the herd, and we are not to worry?" Jones asked.

"That's what he said, Jones, and—he also mentioned my horse is lying back there dead. Best dang horse I ever had," Miller grinned, and Jones sighed.

Getting JD upon his big horse was a chore. Once he was in the saddle, his head began to spin, and he leaned over and retched.

"Abel, you and Jones have to take JD back. I will trail along behind and keep coming. JD needs some doctoring and a place to lie up for a few days. Bring me that big sorrel when you come back. There's no sense in us arguing about this. Jones, if you don't hold JD in the saddle, he will take a fall, and that will definitely finish him off," Miller said.

Abel grumbled to himself, "Jones, Miller is right. There is no other way. It will take most of the day to get back to camp. I will return with some fresh mounts." Looking around, Abel considered every direction.

7

"Look, boss, we come to get one man, and we're leaving another. I don't think this is a good plan," Jones said.

"Miller, follow us back along the way until you come to where the deep gully cuts the prairie. You can hide there. I will be back before dark looking for you there. It's the only place you won't be on the skyline on these plains. If you have to run, move along the gully until you get into the mountains over that away. If I don't find you out here, I will backtrack you into the mountains. Let that be our plan. Cal Lacy told me he found a fast-flowing stream just a few miles east of that mountain range over there. This morning, I crossed the tracks of a buffalo herd on my way here. Remember, where there are buffalo, there are Indians," Abel said.

By noon Miller had reached the gully. Rundown cowboy boots are not suitable for long walks. Upon reaching the gully, he sat down. His eyes followed the gully across the plains, mentally calculating the distance. A depression that had probably started years before as a buffalo wallow was now a deep depression. It collected runoff water from several directions during the rainy season. The depression emptied into a gully that crawls toward the southeast. A small cluster of cedar and mesquite trees lent a splash of green to the winter-brown landscape.

Grumbling to himself, Miller considered the position of the sun. Abel and Jones should be getting JD back to camp. Behind him, a distant whinny of a horse made the hair on the back of his neck stand up. Sliding down in the depression, Miller turned to see if his worst fears had been realized. He drew in a sharp breath.

Several hundred mounted Indians were headed his way a mile or so back. Their scouts had no doubt found the buffalo tracks. *This is about the worst place I can possibly be at this moment!'* he surmised. On all fours and dragging his rifle by the barrel, Miller crawled, and half ran down the wash, raising his head occasionally to see if there was any change in their direction.

I'm too old for this!' Miller whispered under his breath. His trek had taken him to a deeper level of the wash where he could stand up and run. Voices were getting louder. They were almost upon him. He was getting frantic, looking desperately for a place to hide. A deep washout under the bank that looked like it would cave in at any moment offered the only hiding place in sight. Sitting in the depression, he pulled his knees up against his chest. Above him, the sound of horses and Indians talking covered any frightful sound he might have made.

Checking the load in his rifle, he readied himself for one final defiant battle and said a quick prayer. Being taken alive was not an option, and he was too old to run anymore. Something rubbed against his leg and almost gave Miller heart failure. Beside him was Jones' old dog, Bob, shivering from fright and whimpering loudly.

"Shut up, Bob! You want to get us scalped?" Miller grabbed the old dog's muzzle. The two sat quietly, trembling, for above them, hundreds of Indians rode on the plains. Some rode so close to the edge, dirt and grass crumbled and rolled down the bank onto Miller's head. The warriors never knew that below them, separated by only a few feet, an old White man and a dog crouched in stark fear. Finally, they passed, intent on the winter hunt for meat. He let them get out of sight before he stood and made his way along the wash.

Later that day, just before sunset, Miller sat on the bank of a fast-flowing stream, soaking his aching feet. Jones' cow dog lay beside him, fast asleep. *'Abel would see the dust cloud and would know it was Indians looking for the buffalo,'* Miller reasoned. It was a serene moment, total silence except for the gurgling sound of the water and birds singing in the trees. Never had he come so close to death. On this day, Abraham Trent Miller had been spared by the grace of God. He had experienced what Modena had found at the end of his life. Bowing his head, he gave thanks. Life may end tomorrow, but for now, he knew the meaning of mercy. Hundreds of warriors rode the prairie and mountain trails between him and the camp.

In death, Modena's deathbed conversion had made a profound impression on Miller's life. Right now, he only knew that every breath he took was precious, and death was only a victory if you knew the God of the Bible.

C02 - A Personal Matter

William knelt and took a long drink from a stream of fast running water. Raising his head, he whispered. "They're still back there, aren't they?"

Running Deer looked up from filling their water skin. "Their back there, and my intuition tells me it's Black Hawk. We are a personal matter to him. Not only did you get away, but you made him lose face by coming into camp and stealing me away. He will not let up until he has captured us. If he's successful, I promise you we will not be taken back alive," she said.

Leaning back on the sandy bank, William closed his tired eyes and listened to the water rushing over the limestone stream. "This is a pleasant place. I could close my eyes and sleep for a week," he said.

"I fear that if we slept for just a few minutes, Black Hawk would wake us," Running Deer stated.

"Then we better keep moving. Which direction do you want to go?" William asked.

"We will go north. We have crossed signs of the buffalo. The Osage will go after the herd for their winter meat and hides," Running Deer said.

It was growing dark when the two jumped from stone to stone, leaving the stream. "My feet are just about frozen. I don't want to get back in that cold water if I don't have to," William said.

"I don't think we will fool Black Hawk, but he will have to search a long time to find out whether we went up or down and where we left the stream," Running Deer said.

Moving up the side of a rocky slope, they could not keep their teeth from chattering. "We need to find shelter and get warm," William said.

"Tomorrow, we must find food," she said.

A low group of cedar bushes solved the shelter problem. Crawling in among the low-hanging branches, they found a spot where leaves and needles offered a readymade bed. The wind howled, but it didn't penetrate the thick cover they had. Unrolling the heavy buffalo robe, they quickly got in a fold, and almost instantly, William could hear Running Deer's soft breathing. Pulling her close, he relaxed his tired aching muscles and prayed for Divine help. His mind went back to a better time when a warm smile from the faces of his father or mother was his for just a look in their direction.

'How unwise are those who do not recognize the warmth and love of a Christian family,' he thought. William had matured in

his struggle for life while in the wilderness. Now he had found the love of his life. He had to be careful not to dwell on her beautiful face, less he become careless.

A noise woke William in the early morning hours. He was not alarmed because he knew that Running Deer had heard the noise and had only snuggled closer to him.

Pulling her closer, he kissed the back of her head, and the two listened for a long time before she whispered to him, "There are buffalo out on the prairie over there. I figure every brave in the Osage tribe is at the base of this mountain. The hunt will start at first light. They will not be looking for us, and it may be possible we can get meat."

William whispered in her ear, "I think we need to get out of here as fast as possible. Maybe Black Hawk will be distracted from us for a while. It might give us a chance to get away."

"We will not get far unless we eat. We have rested, but our bodies need nourishment. It's been two moons since we have had anything to eat. Longer if you don't count those two small raw fish as a meal. Today we must eat and eat well," she said.

The two dozed for the next two hours, and by early light, they could see the Indians out across the long prairie chasing the buffalo herd. Carcasses of slain buffalo began to dot the open prairie. A kill not too far from the edge of the cedars caught their eyes. "When the squaws finish stripping the carcass, we can get pieces of meat without being seen. Watch over there, William. Do you see the horse-drawn travoises? I have worked on many hunts. The squaws will go to the kill and skin out the carcass. The hide will be loaded on one travois and the meat and fat on another. It will be hauled to their winter camp where the meat will be dried, and the hides scraped and tanned," Running Deer explained.

"That's quite an operation. How do you intend to get close to a kill without being recognized?" William asked.

Running Deer looked around the prairie and studied each site where a kill was being dressed. "The squaws are almost finished with the kill by the gully. We will wait until they move far away from the kill. They are in a hurry and leave good meat hanging on the carcass. We can get meat from what's left behind," Running Deer said.

Each animal carcass was covered by many squaws, and it took only a few minutes until the skeletal remains lay bare on the open plains. The herd moved along the prairie, being herded by Indian ponies trying to keep them close to where the squaws were working the carcasses. Slowly they moved away from the mountain where the two sat watching from their hiding place.

"Okay, William, we can get to that carcass over there and see what meat is left. Right now, I will not be too picky," Running Deer said.

At the first carcass left by the squaws, Running Deer quickly cut small pieces of meat. William began to collect the pieces she cut and placed them in a rabbit skin sack. Occasionally, he would look up and scan the surrounding grassland. He became interested in watching the Indian squaws that worked on the distant carcasses. "That's about it for this animal. Looks like we have a lot of meat," Running Deer said.

The next carcass was even better than the first, and it wasn't long until they had several pounds of small chunks. Suddenly she froze, and her knife stopped cutting. She did not move, and William was instantly alarmed. The two had been so intent on the meat they had become careless. Shadows had fallen over the two. Without turning, they knew it was the shadows of two warriors. Feathers from their hair blew in the wind. The braves stood just a few feet behind them, both with tomahawks ready to strike. Running Deer continued to cut as if they should be there cutting the leftover meat. The problem was that William's brown hair was a dead giveaway no matter how long.

"Blue Dog, you not get away again," one brave stated.

William recognized the voice and a young face flashed through his mind. It was the face of an Indian boy he had ridden with to the trapper's cabin. He remembered his face being twisted with anger and hate as the young braves had plunged knives into the old trapper ending his life. William did not intend to take another beating and die a slow death. Sighing deeply, he looked at Running Deer and said in broken English, "I love you, and knowing you has been worth all the anguish I have suffered."

His turn was unexpected and quick. The young brave was not a seasoned warrior, and knowing the White captive, he didn't expect William to attack. They had been friends and rode together the night William had dishonored himself at the trapper's cabin. His jump back was not quick or far enough, and William's knife went into his chest between the red streaks that signified he was a member of Black Hawk's band.

It would have been a futile gesture on William's part had it not been for the old man who had been watching from his hiding place. Miller had seen the two crawling up to the carcass and knew they were the White Indians who had helped JD. He had seen what they had not seen. Two braves had been stalking them. Before the second brave could raise his tomahawk, he went down from a single shot that echoed across the plains.

Miller figured he owed them plenty for helping his friend. He had been too far back to help as he watched the braves close in on the unsuspecting pair. His only choice was to shoot. Taking careful aim, he was surprised when the White Indian suddenly turned and sent a knife deep into one of the braves making his choice a little easier.

William and Running Deer were shocked to see the second brave fall before them. They were startled when the old cowboy with a dog rose from the brush. Across the plains, occasional shots were heard, but few eyes turned, thinking it was just another buffalo to be skinned.

"It might be really wise if we get out of here in a big hurry," Miller said as he came to where the two sat. William had already taken the dead warriors' weapons. Together they quickly pulled the bodies out of sight.

Running Deer led the way back to the stream and quickly stepped into the fast-moving water. "How far do you think we are from the cow camp?" she asked.

"Twenty or thirty miles away, I reckon," Miller said.

"We will walk in the water for a while, then go into the wilderness," she said.

Miller threw his saddlebags and bedroll over his shoulders. "You young folks lead the way, and I will bring up the rear. You seem to know how to survive in the wilderness. I'm just a cowpuncher, wishing I had a horse under me," he said.

"Don't leave a track or break a branch. They must not know which direction we went. It might be better for you to walk in the middle, so William can make sure you don't leave a track," Running Deer suggested.

Miller chuckled, "I've been in the wide-open spaces all my life and never learned to cover my tracks. I guess I better learn mighty fast, or I might get us all killed,"

They walked for miles in the cold stream before heading into a rocky, pine-covered mountain range. Little was said. They all focused on getting as far away from the prairie as possible before the dead braves were found. Finally too tired to move any further, Miller sat down on the edge of a small stream. It was a picturesque place. Above them, a snow-covered mountain stretched into the evening sky.

Pulling his boots off, Miller stuck his aching feet in a clear pool of water that formed below a waterfall. "Now, this is a great place to rest. You two find some sticks to build a fire, and I will get us a campsite setup," he said.

There were piles of rocks to build a fire pit, and a readymade lean-to jutted out of the mountainside. Plenty of firewood sticks and tree limbs lay around, and they had gathered enough fuel to last a week in no time. Miller selected a well-concealed place to build the fire pit so the firelight would not be detected from a distance. The campsite had a natural windbreak. It wasn't long until the three sat warming themselves, eating chunks of roasted buffalo meat.

Then it struck Miller, *'Where had Jones' old dog Bob, gotten off to? The last time he saw Bob, he was eating meat from a carcass on the prairie. Well, he could tell Jones he had seen his dog!'* Miller thought.

Miles behind them, the bodies of the two warriors had been found. Old Bob watched from a distance, and instincts told him he had worn out his welcome. Smelling the ground, he circled the carcasses and then walked along the small stream. A warrior stood watching the dog track, notched an arrow, and he drew back only to be stopped. "Don't kill! Dog belongs to White-eyes. We follow dog," Black Hawk said.

Jones watched the speck getting larger out on the prairie in the fading evening light. Shaking his head, he walked away from the group, watching Abel return. Behind Abel, the sun slipped below the prairie's edge as he rode into camp.

Leather creaked as he dismounted and trailed the two horses up to the circle of men around the campfire. Accepting a cup of coffee, Abel looked over at Jones. "Jones, I couldn't get to him," he said.

"Abel, I'll take care of your horses," Cal said. Taking the reins, he led the mounts away to the remuda. Cal listened from a distance as Abel explained why Miller did not ride in with him. Taking a sip of the hot coffee, he looked around at the faces of those who had waited for their return.

"Boys, I made it as far as a big boulder sitting in the middle of the prairie. It was my good fortune to have moved into a stand of pines to water the horses. They were loud. I heard them coming long before I was able to see them. There are several hundred Indians out on that prairie now. They are chasing a large herd of buffalo. Miller must have seen them long before they saw him and skedaddled. Fortunately, Miller and I decided if something like this happened, he was to head for a stream that Cal had scouted and then into the mountains beyond. We must get around that tribe out on the prairie to get to him. Right now, I believe Miller is in a much better situation than we are. He is on the other side of the Osage nation where we need to be," Abel said.

Cal walked back to the campfire and got a cup of coffee. "Abel, our most pressing problem is out there in the dark. There are several old bucks scouting our present location. I think the chief sent them because they are of no use hunting the buffalo. Evidently, the chief is not in too big of a hurry to deal with us. By now, the scouts know our weaknesses and how many there are of us. The hunt for winter food is their highest priority. In a few days, that will change," he said.

"Miller is not the only one back there. There are two children, a girl and a boy somewhere on this prairie," JD said. "They helped me—they saved my life and then disappeared last night," JD said.

Jones moved up to the campfire after making a circle around the herd. "The herd is grazing and content, but we have a problem back there. That crazy horse of JD's is mighty upset. There must be Indians coming over the rim behind the herd. They will stampede the herd over us when it gets dark," Jones stated.

Abel looked around at the men standing around the fire. Throwing his coffee in the fire, he said. "Boys, this changes things. Hank, we will move the herd just like we discussed. Get your young braves and as we bring the herd out of the bowl, have them move along each side of the herd. My drovers will show them how to keep the cattle moving. We start moving the herd right now," Abel said.

In a few minutes, Hank had the young braves sit on each side of the canyon opening. The old members of the tribe had been ready to travel for days.

"Abel, the tribe will fall in behind the herd after the dust settles. My father will be leading them. The camp is ready to move. I will take my scouts out front with Cal. We will scout ahead for the best route and a good campsite each night," Hank said.

Abel scratched his chin and looked at the setting sun. "Jones, start them drifting out of the bowl. Get that old lead steer out front and keep him moving. Cal, you and Hank wait for the warriors that come out behind the cattle. They will try and get our remuda. They must not get our horses," Abel said.

Moving forward, a warrior lay low along his horse's back. The trail broke herd had started following the lead steer, and the horses were moving along with the herd out of the bowl. Two days of rest had made them ready to start trailing again. Hank was the first to see the brave among the horses moving slowly out of the bowl valley. He motioned, and Cal acknowledged that he saw the Indian also. Hank was closest and disappeared among the moving cattle. The Indian seemed to rise up and then slipped from view. Hank grabbed the mane of the nearest horse. Clicking his tongue, he moved his mount around with his hands until he had slowed the progress of the remuda. Another Osage brave fell from the side of the bowl without making a sound.

One of Hank's braves mounted and moved around close to Hank. "A big horse is acting up back there. I can't get close to him. He will spook the herd," he said in the Indian dialect.

"That's JD's horse. He is a bit skittish and hates Indians. We are Indians! Cal, you will have to get a rope on that crazy horse, or he will stampede the whole bunch," Hank said.

After a few tense moments, the drovers got control of the horses. Hank and two of his braves went back into the bowl and rooted out another old brave waiting in hiding. It didn't take long to get the herd on the trail moving northwest. Hank rode forward with his braves to scout. Following the cattle, the ragtag tribe of Indians with Hank's family moved in behind. Several old Indians with weapons hung back to help in case there were more Osage to harass them from behind.

"Boss, you need to ride back there and see this. At least fifty Indians are tagging along as a rear guard. Hank's mother and wife are helping Cleve with the wagon, and Lordy, I think we have a cook. There is a bunch of Indian kids herding our cattle with spears. I tell you, it's a sight to see! We need more horses and pack animals for this bunch, but—" Jones said.

"But what?" Abel asked.

"But all-in-all, we are in pretty good shape for the mess we're in," Jones said with a grin.

"Well, we're moving. I would have never believed I would have seen anything like this. With the new calves, we are up to around four hundred head of good stock." Abel looked up at the big moon and frowned. "Jones, if the Indians attack, they will hit the tribe behind us first and kill every last one of our rear guard, men, women, and children. After daylight, I want you to get the drovers to stop the herd and have Professor Lightfoot move the tribe ahead of the herd," Abel said.

Jones eyed Abel for a minute and smiled his approval. "Boss, if Miller was here, he would tell me, '*You know, Jones, for a youngster, the boss sure has his priorities in the right order!*'"

"Jones, I miss Miller's wisdom, too. Be glad when we get him back. I sure have been praying hard for his safety," Abel said.

They both looked out along the prairie in the morning mist and thought their own thoughts. Jones' thoughts were that he hadn't taken the time to pray for his friend as the boss had.

Miles away, Bald Jo Kline stood in a readymade camp sight. He was tired of this game. Chief Ragin Bull was not far away, and there was the White man's whisky. Thunder cracked, and lightning shot across the mountains. Bald Jo stood and looked around at the clouds and said, "Rain comes! Too dark to go up mountain. We make camp here." As evening closed, he considered going hungry tonight. There was plenty of firewood stacked and a good dry shelter for the night. Looking at the other braves, he said. "Dog no help after rain—You follow dog and find man bring him here. Bring dog we eat."

αααααααα

"Cal, winter is coming on with a vengeance. If we don't get south—I mean far south—the way they are dressed, the entire tribe will freeze. I have been praying about it, but for the life of me, I don't see any answer coming. I know you have a good standing with the Lord; see what you can do!" Abel said.

Turning, Cal considered what the boss had just ordered him to do and grinned. "Abel, I will surely put it to prayer for you. Let's put Hank's best warriors on horseback just in case we get in a running fight with the Indians," Cal said.

Abel looked around and pulled the collar up on his old coat. "Okay, work that out with Hank. Well, here we are headed in a northerly direction just when cold weather begins," Abel said.

"I know, boss, but just two more days, and we will be able to turn west then south unless I can find a route southward sooner. Right now, all we need is some space between the Osage and us," Cal said.

Waving goodbye, Abel rode to the front to find the chuck wagon. He wanted to check on JD and get a cup of coffee. *'Finally,'* Abel thought, *'there was someone with this outfit that could make a decent cup of coffee!'* Hank's mother had taken over the cooking, and with Cleve's help, there were no complaints from the men.

Across the mountain, the rumble of approaching rain sent a cold wind that laid the long dry prairie grass over. Looking around at the abandoned Indian camp along the stream as they passed, Abel thought, *This would be a nice place to live. I can see why the old guard hated to leave. Hank and his family did a lot of good for this tribe. Most of the young men and boys were learning English. Professor Lightfoot had purposed to help this tribe and I mean to help too. Now they have convinced the tribe to come with us. If they stayed, the Osage would destroy the tribe. They would never be able to live in peace. Hank's mother and father have the right idea. The only hope of keeping the tribe in existence is to educate them in Biblical values and the ways of the White man.'*

C03 - Miller's Revelation

Miles away, Miller rubbed his aching legs and looked up at the vast mountain range. "There is no way I can climb that. I'm too old and have been bucked off too many broncs. I'm slowing you kids down. It would be better if you went on ahead and left me behind," he said.

William moved back and sat down on a rock, resting for a minute. Running Deer had made it to a ledge a few yards ahead and sat looking out over their back trail. "Mr. Miller, we have already had this discussion, and we are not leaving you. We are making good time," she said.

Miller noticed the look on her face betrayed her last words. "When the rains come, it will wash out our tracks, and we will turn and head in that direction. Black Hawk will not be able to follow in the rain," Running Deer stated.

"That's wishful thinking, and you both know it! It looks like we are going to travel all night. Tomorrow morning, if we are not in a good downpour, I'm changing directions. You well know, I'm leaving a trail a blind Indian could follow," Miller said.

The three sat roasting buffalo meat when William said, "Running Deer, this is about the best meal I have had in a long time." Getting no response from her, William gave Miller a questioning look.

Running Deer seemed remote, looking across the hills. A few more pieces of meat, then she looked again. The sight of her concerned William, for he knew she alone could keep them alive.

Miller stretched and groaned. "The sun is coming up. I would like to stay in this spot. It is the best camping spot we could have. My old cautious nature gives me a different feeling. I fear we are going to have company. You might say I'm overly cautious, but I don't have a good feeling," Miller said.

Running Deer looked around at the campsite and out along the hills again. She didn't say anything for a long time, then suddenly she added all the cooked meat to her pack and said, "Dog comes—warriors follow him!"

Miller sat stunned for a minute, then jumped to his feet. "I should have killed that worthless mutt. Old Bob will get us killed for sure. Nothing will get him off my trail," he said irritably.

"We go now—no way to get away from dog. He will track us until he finds us, and Black Hawk will follow him to us!" Running Deer said.

"I will stay back and shoot that mangy mutt while you two make a run for it," Miller said.

"No, Mr. Miller, now we go—go quickly!" Taking a piece of meat from the pack, she pushed it far up under a boulder and packed rocks in front of it," No one had to ask what she was doing. The only thing that would slow Bob down was the scent of food. Digging it out would take him a few minutes, and every minute would count.

"We need to head that a-way," Miller pointed to the range where Abel would be looking for him.

Full of good meat and needing rest, the three wished for a good night's sleep, but with a dog following them, they would likely not see rest for a long time. The old dog was about the worst thing that could happened to them. Running Deer was downcast. Thinking, *'She could outsmart the Indians and keep them all alive, but she couldn't get away from the dog.'*

Miller sat down on a boulder and rubbed his sore knees. "Running Deer, it doesn't matter how fast we travel. We can't outsmart that dog. Old Bob has my scent and will keep on coming. If we split up, the dog will follow me. We just keep climbing and switching this way and waiting for your rain to come. I'm going that away," Miller said, pointing his walking stick. Bound and determined, he gave the two a sideways look.

"We need to stay together and keep trying to throw Black Hawk off our trail," William said.

"Well, it's not working. He's still back there, and by this time tomorrow, Bald Jo Kline will be walking along with us. You two would have been long gone and to safety if you had just left me behind. Now, this is my plan. That big Injun is not interested in me. He knows I will be headed back to the herd like a bee to a hive. He can wait on me. It's you he wants. We split up, making his tracking much harder, and old Bob will follow me. What do you say we make it a little harder for him? William, you take my rifle and shells pouch. I have my pistol and plenty of shells. Just let me go. I make better time if I travel at my own pace," Miller said.

Running Deer sat and looked at the old man for a long time. "It may be that if we split up, we could stand a better chance of staying alive. They would send a couple of warriors after you. The rest would follow Black Hawk," Running Deer said.

"Then it's settled. That's the direction I will get back to the herd," Miller said.

Running Deer thought for a moment and studied the mountain tops. "Mr. Miller, do you see that mountain top over there?" she asked.

Miller squinted through tired, bloodshot eyes and said, "Now that is a mighty fir piece. I had rather go down toward the prairie and find the herd."

"Mr. Miller, this is the wilderness. If you don't get your bearings, you will wander all over the place. So, listen!" she said, pointing. "When you get to the foot of that mountain, you will be able to see the prairie. If you get there, you may be able to see the herd on the prairie below you. I want you to promise me that you will not give up just because the going gets rough," Running Deer said.

"It's a mighty long walk, but I guess I will try," Miller said.

"No—that's not a promise. You must promise that you will get there," Running Deer said.

Miller looked around at the two. They had both become sturdy and strong with the rigorous life they lived. Miller's face took on a look of resolve. "Yes—for you kids, I promise to make it come hell-or-high-water. I will get there," Miller said.

Suddenly, Running Deer burst into a grin. "You will do it! Now we must leave! Watch for the braves that Black Hawk sends after you and head around the right side of the mountain," she said.

Earlier that day, Old Bob had dug the meat out from under the boulder and moved on following the scent of his old friend. The smell of the two Indians tracking him had hurried him along as fast as his old legs could carry him.

Miller watched the two head away in the opposite direction. These two knew hardship, danger, and the threat of death. *'It is evident and easy to spot they both had good raising. Their upbringing was helping them through the worst possible situation a young person could be in. As for me, my life is one for the books,'* he thought. *'It has not amounted to much. Left home at an early age. Always satisfied with a meager day-to-day existence. Pushing cows, drinking in bars along the trail, and night after night reliving the meaningless, endless tales of little to no substance around the campfires of my life.'* He remembered how Cal would get out a book and read by candlelight each night. He had seldom read a book and could never remember darkening the door of a church. He remembered the Sunday mornings in the towns of his life. The church bells, the singing. These things he had always pushed out of his mind. Someday, when he felt like it, he would investigate the need of his eternal soul. This had been his life. He was learning a lot about life lately, now that he was wrestling to keep it. Life was a struggle, nothing but ups and downs. He had not made a useful difference in his life, but he would surely try from now on. Turning, he sighed and made his way along the most accessible pathway, using the mountain ahead as his guide. He didn't bother trying to cover up his tracks.

Two days passed, and Miller reached some high ground. Rubbing his parched lips, he needed water in the worst way—what he would have given for a canteen full of water. Before him was a vast landscape of valleys and hills; after them were more valleys and higher hills. His movement was slightly upward around the mountain range. He made his way along the peak's right side, hoping to see the prairie below with a herd of whiteface cows just around the next hill. He had eaten the last of his meat two days before, and his backbone was chewing on his belly button. He made camp by a dry riverbed. A large tree nourished by the good water supply most of the year sat near the riverbed. Looking at the cut banks, there was no doubt there had been many flash floods. Miller sighed and considered a small hole at the base of the tree. It could be a rabbit hole, a badger, or maybe a snake hole. Taking his old leather gloves from his pocket, Miller mumbled to himself. *'Well, it's too cold for snakes. So, if I pull one out of this hole, it will be too cold to strike—I think—maybe so. That would be better than a badger. Lord, help me if it's a badger.'* Lying down on the ground, he took a deep breath and reached arm's length into the hole. His hand grabbed something that moved. It was something furry, and after a tug-of-war, he pulled a great big rabbit out of the hole.

As dark fell, the plump rabbit hung golden brown on the spit. It smelled wonderful. He was so intent on the rabbit he had almost forgotten a bunch of mean Indians might follow him. He would have his first meal in two days in a few more minutes. He was becoming wilderness smart, and a slight sound came to him from the darkness. He kept his fire low, but now he threw a few more sticks on the fire to increase the light and moved away into the darkness. He hated leaving the fire, especially the rabbit, but he moved far back in the timbers and rocks. By his campfire, two shadowy figures moved just out of the firelight. Suddenly, he had the oddest thought. He had not asked God to send the rain Running Deer had prayed for. Below him, one fierce-looking Indian darted into the firelight and scooped up his supper. Now he would not have supper even if he lived through the night. Bowing his head, he quietly prayed, *'Lord, I remember my sin. I should have prayed for rain to cover our tracks, just like Running Deer did. I might add that I need help to stay alive and am mighty hungry and thirsty. Amen!'*

The wind took on a damp smell, and a gentle rain swept the mountain range. On occasion, the two shadows were only visible from heat lightning far above the mountain. The rain fell high up on the mountain, and an actual lightning storm came. Deftly the braves moved around the campsite, working in and out of the boulders looking for the old cowboy. They stopped close enough Miller could hear them whispering. He didn't understand what they were saying, but he understood they would not eat until they had finished the old White-eyes. They wrapped the rabbit in animal skin and laid it beneath a flat rock a couple of feet in front of Miller.

Up the mountain, rainwater began to move down the mountainside and along the dry riverbed. At first, in small ribbons. Then the ribbons swelled and combined with other streams as it came. Faster and higher, it came bouncing off the boulders. Miller noticed his hiding place just happened to be shielded from the enormous amount of water that had been funneled along the small stream. Quickly he eased out in the rain and retrieved the rabbit. It was still warm, wrapped in the animal skin. Scooting back into his hiding place, he watched as the two Indian warriors were bowled over and swept downstream, fighting for their lives.

Miller ran his hand over the soft, warm animal skin that held his meal and considered if what he had just witnessed could have possibly been true. Then he realized that the animal skin was actually an empty waterskin. Now he had a water pouch to carry water. *'Could it be that I have lived a life not knowing the God that would show such mercy and watch care? Even to someone who had never given his creator a thought? Lord, you are God, and with your help, I will do my best to finish well. Keep them safe and help them survive,'* Miller prayed.

Grinning from ear to ear, Miller sat eating the best meal he could remember. Suddenly he caught movement out of the corner of his eye. Turning, he frowned. there sat Old Bob waiting for his share of the rabbit. "Well, Bob, you brung a couple of savages to kill me, and now you want me to feed you," Miller said.

Miles south travoises laden with buffalo meat and hides made their way across the prairie. Tonight, there would be a great feast to sing and dance to the gods of the buffalo hunt. While not far away, the rescue of Miller and the hunt for William and Running Deer continued.

C04 - Broken Reckoning

Jericho Dawson limped along a small river's edge a few miles upstream. He stopped for a breather and drank from the clear water and listened to the stream gurgling and splashing along. Jericho's ears were keen to the sounds of the forest. Behind him, his pack mule stood restless. This Jenny was wilderness smart. She could smell Indians better than any he had ever had. Tonight, she was upset, and her ears were twitching and turning.

He would be in the Crow's Nest in just a mile more. It was a fortified trading post where he had spent many a night haggling over the price of a pile of furs. He was sure he hadn't been detected. There were Indians around; he had seen signs. He would bet a silver dollar they were getting ready to make war on the trading post.

Pike Smithers ran the post and refused to leave. He would be there for sure. The Indians had left him alone for the simple reason he sold them whisky. Black Hawk had been one of his frequent customers.

Reaching the lodge, Jericho whistled, and a lantern light was waved in front of a gun port. Jericho's bad leg wasn't slowing him down when he crossed the clearing and entered as the door swung open.

"Strip her pack and run her out the door. She will fare better on her own this night!" Jericho said. Behind him could be heard leather straps being cut. Swiftly the door was opened, and the little mule took off running into the night.

"Dawson, it sure is good to see your ugly mug this night, but I don't see how you made it here," Pike said.

"They're out there, Smithers, and they didn't come to trade," Jericho replied.

Looking around the lodge, Pike had stationed three men, one on each side of the building. Jericho acknowledged each of the trappers and was greeted kindly in return.

"How many you reckon Dawson?" Pike asked.

"We are dealing with a lot of Indians out there tonight. I reckon there may be a hundred or more," Dawson stated.

"I sure hope you are wrong, Jericho," Joe Creech said.

"I wish I was, Big Joe. There are so many out there in the dark they're falling over one another," Jericho said.

"Which brings me to the question. I heard you had left the mountains cause of this Indian trouble. What brought you back?" Pike asked.

"You boys all knew the Irishman, Clay Murphy, and his wife Etta that lived over by the Wishbone?" Jericho asked.

"We all knew that family. Which of us has not had a good meal cooked by Etta. It grieved us all that they came to a bad end. I hear that was Kline's work. He's a bad one. I hope he ain't standing in the dark just outside this building," Pike said.

"Well, it seems their boy William Murphy is alive. They took him captive and had been making an Injun out of the lad," Jericho Dawson said. "His uncle is up here in the mountains looking for the boy. I hope to help William get clear of them Skins if I can," Jericho Dawson said.

"Jericho, you are just a wishing. Likely, the boy is dead, and it would have been merciful if they had killed him knowing what they would have done to him," Pike said.

"That's true, but I think I'm right, and I'm obliged to try. How are you boys set on powder and shot?" Jericho asked.

"I have three kegs of powder in the cellar. There is enough powder and shot with all these weapons leaning around the walls to carry us through the night. These boys are all good shooters. I guess you and I will stand and load for them,"

"Pike, how big is that cellar in your floor?" Jericho asked.

Big Joe replied, "It's a fair size storeroom now. I got it all timbered and shored up a month ago. I usually keep canned goods, furs, and my powder kegs down there. Right now, it's full of my year's fur trading. Why you ask, Jericho?"

A shot rang out from outside, and Big Joe Creech folded and dropped to the floor. The other men returned fire, shooting into the darkness. "Hold your fire, boys. You are wasting lead," Jericho and Pike looked at the body lying on the floor.

"Pike, turn off that lantern. Big Joe is done for. Let's move him out of the way. That was a Sharps rifle, and only one Indian I know can shoot a buffalo gun that well in the dark," Jericho said.

"Yep, that's Ragin Bear out there, and he never travels without plenty company," Pike said.

"Well boys, we're going to have a long night. Don't get careless, and let's make them pay for every scalp they collect," Pike said.

Far back in a clearing, a campfire was surrounded by the best of Ragin Bull's warriors and just as many of Black Hawk's braves. "Black Hawk come because you sent for him," Jo Kline snarled. "Why you not listen to me? My medicine strong, Chief Ragin Bull, why you not listen?" Black Hawk asked.

Chief Ragin Bull stood on the other side of the campfire and raised his hand, saying, "Tonight, my medicine strong. Great Spirit will give me great victory over trading post. You and warriors fight. I lead war on post this night! We make war and take many scalps and much booty White man has in trading post!"

Black Hawk looked at his band. He was not pleased that the only place he could get liquor would soon be gone. "I not fight this night! It's no good to destroy the trading post. My Medicine strong and I fight…your warriors follow me this night. We get much buffalo and beaver pelts." Black Hawk made a sign and his followers moved to the front of the line next to Ragin Bull. Their strength made it clear they would be first in the trading post. Following their chief Ragin Bull in this battle, they gave out a war cry, and all moved through the dark woods. Ragin Bull thought, *This night I will regain the respect of all the tribes as it has been in the past.*

Black Hawk smoldered in the darkness and watched from a distance.

For hours the battle raged. Inside the cabin, everyone was gasping for a good breath of fresh air. The rifles' acrid smell and heavy smoke lingered heavily in the air. Several attempts to break down the heavy door were repelled and cost the attackers dearly. Dead Indians lay around the cabin, and the price for victory was getting higher.

In a lull in the fighting, Jericho leaned his rifle against the wall and coughed. Pouring a dipper of water over his head, he blew his nose and grumbled, "I have been hoping for a shot at that old chief. Just one shot at that old devil would be worth dying for. It's clouding up! We are about to lose our moonlight!"

"Too bad I never finished the tunnel to the river. We would have at least a chance of getting away," Pike said.

"What's that Pike? What tunnel?" Jericho asked.

"In the cellar. I started a tunnel to the river. What I have finished is all shored up with timbers. I figure I have at least ten feet left to go, and it's been mighty hard digging all the way," Pike said.

"How far out from this building have you gone?" Jericho continued to question.

"It's seventy-five feet now. I know what you are thinking, but it will take too long to dig it out in our present situation. It's been hard clay digging all the way," Pike stated.

"What if we dig straight up?" Jericho asked.

Pike grinned, "It's worth a try! Up is about six feet, the depth of a grave. I smell something burning!" Pike yelled.

"The Red devils are setting the roof on fire!" a trapper said.

"Pike, I helped you build this place, and that's a double roof with a foot of dirt between just for this situation. That old chief wants your furs, and before this place burns, they will be coming. The moonlight is about gone. They have the advantage now. If they rush the door, we're done for. I got an idea. Get the kegs of gunpowder and set them against these three main roof supports," Jericho said.

The fighting resumed, and the smoke was getting unbearable. Along the hill above the lodge, fifty warriors carried old limbs and driftwood to throw onto the roof. It wasn't long until they had a roaring fire on the roof. It worked against the braves in that it lit up the woods. The men in the burning building were excellent shots. Their shots hit even the smallest exposed flesh that moved far back in the shadowy woods.

"Jericho, your plan better work, real soon. I don't think I can stand much longer in this smoke and heat. The timbers above us are smoking and about ready to flame up!" Pike yelled.

"Break the legs off the heavy table and lean it up against the cellar door. When we go in, I want it to fall over on top when we close the cellar door," Jericho said.

"It looks like Ragin Bull is getting ready for another rush. Take the bar off the door and prop a chair against it. Now get in the cellar. I hope the old chief leads this charge himself," Pike said.

"Here they come!" a trapper yelled.

Jericho Dawson was the last one and he dove through the small cellar door, jerking it closed behind him. The heavy timber tabletop collapsed over on top of the cellar securing the doom of those in the cellar should the fire last too long. The furs took up most of the storeroom, which displaced the much-needed air supply. The trappers huddled back against the back walls of the cellar and held their ears. Pike lit two candles and handed one to Jericho. Above them, they heard the chair give way, and the door swing open as wild screaming Indians entered the lodge.

"Pike, let's light 'em up!" Jericho said as they each lit a fuse. Pike lit his fuse, then turned and made his way down the escape tunnel, followed by the other three. The lodge exploded as three kegs of gun powder spaced around the lodge ignited, turning the inside of the lodge into an inferno. The ceiling collapsed, pushing a hot blast of smoky air out through the windows and door.

Outside, the remaining Indians staggered around in astonishment and shock. The burning gunpowder flash had singed many braves standing close to the building, and some were thrashing about in the river. Chief Ragin Bull was a fighter and had indeed led the last charge into the lodge. The building was now a heaping pile of burning logs and flesh. In the distance, Black Hawk stood watching the end of Chief Ragin Bull and all of Black Hawk's warriors. His band had been wiped out.

Bald Jo needed a drink of the White man's whisky in the worst way. He no longer had a desire to follow Running Deer.

Below the inferno, the trappers had crawled down the tunnel and dug frantically in the dark. The air was almost gone. Small droplets of fire rained through the cellar door. Pike removed a couple of ceiling boards at the end of the tunnel and, with his shovel, dug a hole straight up. Dirt fell in great chunks around him. Below him, the men were moving armloads of earth back behind them. It was getting hard to breath, and the last man in the tunnel finally lay his head down and went to sleep.

A small grassy knoll hid Pike as he burst through the turf and quickly jumped from the hole pulling Buster Franks behind him. Jericho Dawson was third, and he stood in the tunnel and gasped for a minute before disappearing again to drag Frank Pepper out behind him. The three pulled the unconscious man behind a group of bushes and lay gasping for air.

"He is breathing! We are all alive thanks to you, Jericho!" Pike whispered.

"You better thank the Lord for that. I am as surprised as anyone else we are still pumping air!" Jericho said.

The trappers quietly stood in awe, looking at the flattened trading post. "Wow, would you look at that! From the sound the Indians were making in the trading post over our heads when the powder went off, I'd say there must be a lot of dead Indians flattened in that structure," Pike said.

From their vantage point, they could see the explosion's damage to the lodge. The roof's weight had utterly flattened the inside of the structure, leaving burning log walls still standing. Before crawling away, they watched the dumfounded Indians, some in shock, standing around the smoldering structure.

Jericho knew his wish had come true. Ragin Bear had undoubtedly led the last charge and now lay below the burning timbers. Slowly the Indians moved away from the clearing. The explosion was deafening, and most staggered or wailed from singed flesh. They would return for their dead. Chief Ragin Bull's medicine had been weak. Tomorrow the tribe would mourn a great many of their braves. The loss of Chief Ragin Bull would take away from Black Hawk much of his power and support among the Osage tribes.

Away from the smoldering logs, the rain had cooled the night air, and the trappers were standing in a cold rain.

C05 - Facing Death Straight On

Miller walked along in the cold rain. It had been hours since he had heard the explosion that shook the ground. The river he was following had given him a glimpse of the fire through the woods. He had heard the gunshots and war cries before the explosion, and he changed directions. Crossing the river, he had climbed the side of a hill to get some distance from whatever had happened. Hours later and just about to drop, he crawled in below some thick cedar branches and went to sleep.

A few hours later, soaking wet, he crawled from under the cedar and stood in the cold rain. He scanned the direction he was headed each time lightning flashed. On the side of a mountain, there was a dark spot. It could be a cave or overhanging rock formation. Once again, he trudged along, making his way higher up, hoping to find a dry place to get out of the frigid wind.

Sighing deeply, Miller sat on the windward side of a boulder that partially blocked the wind. Resting there for a minute, he waited in the dark for a lightning flash. The lightning flashes had been his way of keeping himself on course through the night. A strong bolt of lightning to the north assured him he was closer to a point over the prairie where he might see the herd. Trudging along, he grumbled to himself, "I got to get out of this rain!" As if by divine direction, he suddenly stood before a dark hole in the sheer face of a rolling hill. *'Well, it may be a hole full of Indians, bears, or wolves, but if I don't get out of this cold rain, I will die anyway,'* he thought.

Stepping into the dark cave, he instantly realized he was not alone. A strong smoke odor stung his nose, and he eased his pistol out of its holster. Backing against the wall, he stood very still. He could hear the quiet breathing of more than one human.

"Well, say something! I heard you coming a mile away," a sleepy voice said.

"I can smell you, and you talk English. I sure hope you ain't Injun. I'd say you was in that big fire I passed a few hours ago by the smell. My name's Miller. I am a drover what has got separated from the herd I was a driving," he said.

"Nice to meet you, Miller. I suppose you are as cold and wet as we are. Name's Jericho Dawson, and there are four of us. Indians attacked the Crow's Nest Trading Post. There were five of us then. We four got out alive with our scalps, but not much else. I have used this cave for shelter before. We are mountain men all tired out from Injun fighting and being wet and cold!"

"I've heard of you, Jericho Dawson. I'm hoping I have friends somewhere east of here," Miller said.

"Miller, I don't suppose you have a buffalo robe and something to eat on you?" Jericho asked.

"I'm just barely alive and was hoping you might have some food. I am a-figurin' the herd I was pushing is somewhere close by. Tomorrow, I hope to see them from the side of this mountain. They are out there somewhere with a warm fire and plenty to eat if you boys want to come along," Miller said.

αααααα

The following morning Red laid a heavy limb on the campfire and poked at the fire with a blackened tipped stick. "It's hard to get this wet wood to burn," he muttered as Hank rode back into camp. The night sky had cleared, and the sound of cattle bawling permeated the night. The last two days in the saddle had been long. It was evident that Hank was worried.

"Abel, the drovers are bedding the herd down. Cal and two of my braves took four buffalo this morning, so the tribe has plenty to eat today. I had my dad move the tribe over to the south side of the herd. If the herd gets spooked and decides to run, we do not want the tribe in their path," Hank said.

Abel rubbed his chin and said, "Hank, there hasn't been any signs of Indians forward. Reports from the rear are much the same. I don't know what to make of that."

"Don't let your guard down. They are out there." Smiling proudly, Hank said, "The young braves have become proficient at keeping the cattle out of the brush. They are making really good drovers."

"Hank, you and your Indians are doing a fine job. I've never seen spirits so high. So, what else is bothering you?" Abel asked.

Hank sat down on the edge of the fire and crossed his legs. His head was down, and he sat drawing in the dirt. "Abel, I don't know what to do. My family has been meeting each evening and praying, but there is silence from heaven. My old Indians will start to die from exposure to the cold in a few days. The only thing that has kept them alive so far is all the good deer and buffalo meat we have been able to get them. I know that won't last. It will get harder and harder to find meat. When the first winter storm hits these high plains, it will not warm up until spring. I know God kept me alive in the war. I have seen his handiwork in the tough times of my life, but what can He do to keep this tribe alive without winter clothing?" Hank asked.

While they were talking, Cal rode into camp for a fresh mount and some supper. "Abel," Cal said, "I think I have found what we are looking for. It looks to be a good trail south. We're not going to make Linda Joy pass. It's too late. There is a blizzard in the mountains, dropping several feet of snow. If this proves out, I think we can turn south tomorrow. We can let the cold north wind urge the herd on. How about you and I take a ride and see if the way is clear. The boys can turn the herd and follow along after the sun gets up," Cal said.

Abel sipped his hot coffee and considered what Cal had said. "That sounds good to me. My horse is saddled, so let's take a look. We will take extra mounts and ride hard," Abel said. Two hours later, he dismounted his horse by a stream to tighten his girth.

"Boss, take a break here and water and rest our spare horses. I'll go check out the pass south. It should only take me a couple of hours," Cal said.

Abel didn't have to be asked twice. He nodded and sat down on a large boulder to rest. "If it still looks good to you in the daylight. We will be headed south by noon," Abel said. An hour later, Cal was scanning the south pass he had found. Removing his binoculars from his eyes, he smiled and turned his horse for the long ride back.

ααααααα

Black Hawk sat in his buffalo robe staring into his warm fire. Earlier that morning he had lost his band of warriors and sat considering his situation. Osage braves had been raiding south and west of the Missouri, looking for horses to steal. From the information he had been getting, times were changing along the lower prairie. Bald Jo Kline was aware a new day was coming for the Red man.

Many Bluecoats had been seen by the raiding parties. The cavalry was back, and their strength was far greater than he had seen in the past. It was time for him to make a move. The White man's war had freed the slaves, and life in the White man's world would improve for the Black man. He was no more concerned with the White slave and half-breed daughter of Jason Murdock. Tired and cold he would make his way back to camp and rest for a few days. Black Hawk had plans to make. The sound of horses came to him through the trees. Somewhere along this stream were several horses. *'What better way to get back to the camp than ride?'* he thought.

A short walk along the stream, and he made out a White cowboy standing next to three horses switching a saddle from one to another. Easing down on one knee, he watched and sized up his prey.

Abel wiped the red mare down with the saddle blanket and let her drink from the stream. Patting her on the rump, he began saddling a big gelding.

Something didn't feel right to Abel, and he turned swiftly. Before him stood the biggest Indian, he had ever seen with his knife ready to strike. Another few steps, and Bald Jo Kline could have killed him without a sound. They both stood staring at each other. Abel's pistol was tied down, and his rifle was in the saddle scabbard on the ground. They both knew before he could get the pistol out, he would be dead. Instantly he jerked out his knife.

Bald Jo Kline was well armed with a repeater rifle and could have easily just shot Abel, but instead, he just grinned and raised his knife.

"Bald Jo Kline," Abel said.

"You know who me—White-eyes," Jo said.

Abel swallowed hard. "Everyone knows of Black Hawk. Your life is not a story you can be proud of. You are a bad Indian and cause much hurt. People fear you and you make little children cry," Abel said.

"I kill you, White-eyes, and take your horses," Kline said.

A voice from behind him said, "Bald Jo, before you die, I want you to turn around and look at me," Cal said. Instantly

Abel drew his pistol and moved out of reach of the big Indian.

The voice behind Kline took him by surprise. Like a coiled snake, he turned to see Cal sitting on his horse with his rifle to his cheek.

Kline instantly knew the cowboy was out of reach of his knife, but he smiled and hissed, saying, "Now I have to kill you both."

"Before you make a move, I want you to look closely at me. My name is Calvin Lacy—I am your son. Before you kill my friend, you must kill me, your son. I am the papoose you traded for whisky eighteen years ago," Cal said.

Abel was floored, and the look on Kline's face was of total shock. With Cal's declaration, everything froze. Never in Jo Kline's life had anything like this ever happened. He was utterly without words. Sliding his knife back in its sheath, he turned and walked along the stream. His savage life had not equipped him to handle this dramatic moment. Before he disappeared, he turned. For a long time, he stood looking at Cal. It seemed he wanted to make a gesture. Finally, he raised his hand in a sign of peace and disappeared.

Cal placed his rifle back on safety and said, "I could not kill him, Abel. Now you know my secret. No one will ever accept me. The blood running through my veins is the same as that murdering savage

I just let walk away. All these years, I wondered if I would ever meet him, and now it has happened," Cal said.

Abel placed his pistol back in its sheath and picked up his knife. "Cal, I can tell you that I am alive because the son of a savage just saved my life. Had you not been here, I would have surely been killed. My mother would live the rest of her life alone without any family. My fiancé would never know what a wonderful husband I plan on making for her. Many men, women, and children would never sit and hear how God used the son of the meanest man in the west to save my life. They would never hear how you read scripture to a dying man and changed his eternal destination. No one would ever hear how the godly influence of the son of the most feared savage alive has changed the men around him from being fast drinking, hard riding drovers, to men that ask question after question about godly living and salvation. As for me, from now on I have a big responsibility. I must live up to the sacrifice you were willing to make to save me. I must live a life worthy of such a friend as you. Nothing has changed, except I am most grateful to have you as my friend. Let's ride back and meet the herd," Abel said.

As they rode back, Abel said, "A week more of good weather would have gotten us over the pass."

"Well, it would have been a better way than heading south now, but at least we will soon be headed south," Cal said.

"We're about a day or two away from a full-blown blizzard, and we have a big, big problem. Hank's tribe is starting to show signs of cold fatigue. We need to find them shelter and fast. There is not enough wood out here to build them warming fires. We have to have clothing for close to a hundred and eighty Indians, or they will start freezing to death," Abel said.

"When the Osage attack, and they will, they will wait and catch us moving the herd. Then swoop down on the herd and the Bidai tribe while we are all strung out. We can't clothe the tribe and they will be easy prey for the Osage," Cal said.

"What a predicament," Abel said.

"That doesn't leave us any options. Moving this many people in our present condition this time of year puts us in a dangerous position. Without proper supplies and clothing, we are just days away from Indians starting to freeze to death. It's a hard winter that covers these mountains. All the tribes have set up their winter camp with plenty of buffalo meat to eat," Cal said.

At first light, a heavy fog settled across the prairie. It was a cool morning when they rode into camp. Abel rubbed his chin and noted the men around the fire, his eyes contacting each face. Hank Lightfoot was chief of the tribe and stood deep in thought. This problem was unsolvable by human hands. It was an all-consuming problem for Abel. What in the world would he do?

Abel stood and looked at the men around the circle. "I have decided there is only one way to save the Indians. Today we will stop forward movement and start killing the herd. We must turn the hides into winter garments for the Indians. The meat will get us through the winter and the long trip down into the Texas hills as soon as we can travel. We may make it home with a few head," Abel said.

JD had been leaning on the wagon tongue. He had mainly recovered from having a rifle ball bounced off his head. With the aid of a crutch Jones had made, JD walked over to the campfire. Settling down next to the fire, he looked over at Cal. "That boy," he said, indicating Abel, "has turned out to be the man his dad wanted him to be. I just wish there was another way without sacrificing the herd, but there is not. Keeping those cows alive had been a struggle across every mile we have traveled. Abel's heart is in the right place. Cal, I have not had a headache today, so I will be back in the saddle first light and pull duty tomorrow," JD said.

Standing up, Cal eyed the men around the campfire. "Well, men, we all know our predicament. If anyone can add anything that might help this situation, let us know. We need to help the boss develop a winter plan that does not mean butchering his herd. We do have one thing in our favor. When the weather turns freezing cold, the Osage will keep close to their warm teepees. They have plenty of meat and will prefer to wait for a good warm snap to do any fighting," Cal said.

C06 - Provisions Offered

The sun didn't burn away the fog, and the weather added a gloomy feel to the men around the campfire. Jones and Red came in from the night riding early to find a cold group of men gathering around the campfire. Abel buttoned the top button on his coat and looked at the two men with a questioning look. "Boss, get ready for a fight. The Osage are coming. It's too foggy to tell how many, but there is plenty for sure," Jones related.

"I hate to fight before breakfast," JD moaned. Suddenly men scattered around the perimeter and found as much cover as possible. All was quiet as the distant sound of men walking came to their ears. Then came a sound that made all the drovers bow their heads in thanks. "Hello, the camp!" It was Miller's voice that came through the morning air.

"Miller, where in the world have you been! We specked you a week ago. What do you have to say fer yourself?" Jones shouted, wiping tears from his eyes. Suddenly a troop of mountain men led by a smiling Miller walked into the firelight. The bunch was haggard at best but all well-armed and smiling. For the first time in days, Abel smiled as Miller introduced the trappers to the men around the fire.

"Well, we have been expecting a large party of Osage warriors, so you men are a sight for sore eyes," Cal said.

The trappers all grinned at each other, and Pike Smithers spoke up, "I don't think you have to worry about that right now."

Jericho chuckled at seeing Cal, and the two shook hands. "Calvin Lacy, it's been a long time. It's good to see you, Calvin. You've done growed plum up, boy! How's your folks? I sure could use a good dose of Doc's medicine right about now. What you doing on a cattle drive?" Jericho said.

"Jericho, you always did ask too many questions at one time. Dad is fine, and so is mother. Yes, I'm all grown up, and it has been a long time. You know I don't like to be called Calvin. Now, what makes you fellows think we won't be seeing a war party soon?" Cal asked, struggling in the bear hug Jericho was giving him.

All around, the group of mountain men was smiling at each other. Jericho was thoughtful for a few minutes, then said, "Well, they lost their meanest war chief. Chief Ragin Bear went against a trapper's lodge that had been a sore spot to him for years. The post was called the Crow's Nest. It was run by a crusty old trapper by the name of Pike. That be Pike setting over there nursing that cup of coffee. Ragin Bear and Bald Jo Kline are the main troublemakers. Bald Jo refused to war against Pike because it was the only place Kline could get his liquor. Ragin Bear took his best and meanest warriors and attacked night before last. There was five of us trappers in the lodge. The warriors paid a heavy price but still couldn't get to us. So, they set fire to the roof. The roof held because Pike's lodge had a double roof with a foot layer of earth between. With the roof burning, we knew we were doomed."

Jericho was in his element telling a good story. "Outside the post, Ragin Bull rallied his warriors. He wanted the liquor and furs that Pike had in the trading post. While the warriors massed for an all-out attack, we set up some fireworks. Three kegs of black powder were set around the room against the ceiling support timbers. When the braves entered the building, the kegs of powder was lit off. The explosion brought the burning roof down on a great number of warriors, including the chief. No doubt Ragin Bull led the attack. He wanted all to know he was as much a leader as Kline. If we're lucky Bald Jo was with them," Jericho said.

"Well, Abel and I know that Jo was not with Chief Ragin Bull because he was with us," Cal said.

The camp got deathly quiet. "Might you elaborate on just what you mean when you say Bald Jo Kline, the meanest Indian that ever breathed, was with you two youngins? Which don't make sense because you two are still breathing!" Jericho said.

"First, tell me, how did you all get out of the lodge?" Cal asked, knowing the suspense would kill them.

Jericho smiled and continued, "We were all in Pike's cellar when the warriors came through the door. Last spring, Pike dug an escape tunnel, and it for sure saved our lives. With Ragin Bull dead, Bald Jo Kline had lost his main supporter! The other chiefs would not back Kline without Ragin Bull."

"What do you think we should do?" Abel asked.

"If you folks can hold on, the Indian trouble may take care of itself. It may eventually burn itself out. Now if you don't mind, would you explain the earlier statement concerning you two and Bald Jo Kline?" Jericho inquired.

Abel continued his and Cal's story, "Cal found a way south, so we do not have to cross Linda Joy Pass. Yesterday, Cal and I rode ahead to make sure the way was clear. It looks to be a good route. I stopped by a spring to water and saddle up spare horses while Cal scouted the route. I heard a noise and turned to find Bald Jo Kline standing not thirty steps behind me with the biggest knife I ever saw in his hand. A few more steps, and he would have killed me before I even knew he was there," Abel said. Taking up the coffee pot, he poured himself another cup of coffee. "I'm so glad someone in this outfit can make a decent cup of coffee."

Jericho looked at Cal and realized the cat was out of the bag. "Well, Abel, what did you do then?" Jericho asked.

"My rifle was in the saddle holster on the ground, and my pistol was tied down, so I jerked out my knife," Abel said.

Around the campfire, men began to laugh. This story was a big yarn like most of Jericho's seemed to be. "Now, Abel, ain't no man in his right mind going to go against the meanest Indian on the river with a little knife like you got there," Frank Pepper said.

"Well, I saw it with my own eyes," Cal said. "I would not have believed it had I not come up and seen it myself. Bald Jo didn't see me, and he laughed and told Abel what he would do to him. I had the drop on Bald Jo Kline, and we were at a stalemate. I made sure I was not in striking distance of Kline, but it seemed I was still too close looking at Jo. You could have cut the air with a knife," Cal said.

"You were in shooting distance of Jo Kline and didn't empty that repeater into that savage?" Frank Pepper asked.

Cal looked around at Jericho and nodded. Jericho stood up and looked at the men around the campfire. "I guess I better explain a little of what this boy was facing.

I have never told the story. I've held it in for close to nineteen years. Now you boys are a fixin' to hear the story firsthand," Jericho pointed to Pike and Pepper and said, "You two know the story but just haven't put it together in your heads yet."

"Both of you boys were in Jack Spikes trading post the day Jason Murdock braced the then young Bald Jo Kline. Remember Jason bought Kline's squaw and papoose for three jugs of whisky? Well, I want you to meet Calvin Lacy, the papoose that Samantha Lacy was holding that cold winter day. A year earlier, Samantha had been taken when Kline and a war party massacred almost everyone on the Snow wagon train." Around the campfire, everyone stood stunned, letting that sink in.

The morning sun burned the fog away about that time, and Jericho stood looking at the tribe of Indians standing around the herd. Jericho was a very observant man and stood scratching his chin.

"Well, I declare! You cowboys, have yourselves your own tribe of Injuns. That's the Bidai tribe! It comes to mind they might be dressed a might light for this time of year, don't you think?" Jericho asked.

"Jericho, you just touched on my biggest problem. The Osage attacked the Bidai Indian camp a couple of weeks ago. Killed off several of their braves and old folks and burned everything they had. The rest of the tribe escaped with only the clothes on their back. We are about to start killing my herd to feed and clothe them. If we don't, they will surely freeze to death," Abel said.

For a long time, the mountain men stood as the realization settled in on them of the plight of the tribe. Then Pike stood, and his eyes locked on those of Jericho's. "You boys thinking what I'm thinking?" Pike Smithers asked.

Looking at the mountain, the men around him each nodded a yes and grinned back at Pike. Frank Pepper reached in his leather bag and tossed Pike a sack full of coins. "Pike, this might help you offset the loss that's a-comin' to you. I'm alive today because of the mercy of the Almighty, and I want to show my appreciation," Pepper said.

In unison, each mountain man did the same, proclaiming their sentiments of God's mercy and appreciation to Him for being alive. It was a thoughtful moment when the wind blew its cold breath across the plains, and there seemed to be a great sense of understanding among the big silent men.

"Men, I know you all want to have a part in this and want to show your gratitude for God's mercy. I tell you now, I have never known a better stand of men in my life as you boys, and if I had died back there in the trading post, I would have died among the best men God ever created," Pike said with watery eyes.

The punchers stood around trying to figure out what in the world these big mountain men were getting all choked up about and tossing their poke to one man.

"Would one of you four kindly explain what you are talking about?" Abel asked.

"Well, we might have to borrow that wagon and the team of mules, but Pike's storeroom below the burned-out trading post is chuck-full of tanned buffalo robes ready to be made into winter clothing. There's also canned goods, bolts of cloth, and food enough to fill that big wagon a couple of times over," Jericho said.

"Ragin Bull is dead, and I doubt you will see any Indians on the plains for a few days. They won't go anywhere without a chief with strong medicine. I think they are back getting them a new chief and making ready for the first snow," Hank said.

"Let's get this herd moving. We're wasting daylight," Red said joyously, slapping his leg with his hat.

"Tomorrow, at this time, we will be out of Osage territory and on our way to Texas. About the only thing left is we need more horses mighty bad, but I think God probably has that worked out too!" Miller exclaimed.

Abel, astonished by the mountain men's declaration, stood and faced the men. "Hank, inform your Indians the God we worship has not forgotten them and tell them about all that has transpired here. Now let's get this herd moving!" he said.

C07 – Uncertain Future

The Osage tribes were stretched out for miles along the river bank. Bald Jo Kline walked along from camp to camp. The death of Ragin Bull and most of his fierce warriors were the talk in every camp. Black Hawk had lost every single one of his warriors, and he stood as a dethroned chief. No one followed him from camp to camp. All received him with hollow stares as he made his way through each camp. The fact that he was not dead along with Ragin Bull had started rumors that he might be the next chief of Ragin Bull's tribe. His medicine must be strong. That was probably a good rumor among the young warriors but not what Bald Jo had in mind to do. Warriors of Chief Ragin Bull's tribe wanted to make him Chief, but he had a different plan. The uneasy feeling, he now had magnified itself, and he feared his life was the main target of the bluecoats that now covered the land.

At night around the campfires there was much talk. The talk had made him uneasy. The conversation was of large troops of Blue Coats on horseback. There were so many the sun rose and set over their camp. They had been seen along the southern plains. It was only a matter of time before the seasoned fighting men

called the horse soldiers would march onto
the high plains to war with the Indians.

After the setting of the sun, he
quietly slipped away. There was a cave far
down the river with all the booty stored
from the raids he had led over the years. It
was time for him to leave the Indian way
of life. His canoe was large. He had
collected from his victims all the gold and
silver coins and clothing that fit him. Now
he had much of the White man's coins. He
had been wise, and now he was prepared
for just this very day. He would take his
canoe out to the big river and head south.

A cold wind blew the night he sat by
the campfire listening to the old chiefs and
news of the Bluecoats. The cold weather
was coming. It was easy by night to travel
the big river. Jo Kline was beginning to feel
free. He had taken a chest in a raid years
before. The coins alone made the chest
heavy. Late that night, he collected the
chest hidden in his cave and set out down
the swift-moving river.

Jo Kline remembered New Orleans.
That is where he would go. Many Black
people there could help him learn to speak
English again. He smiled to himself. He
had always wanted to ride a paddlewheel
on the great river and walk the streets of
that great city again. Over the years, while
riding along the riverbanks, he had seen the
big sternwheelers moving along the great
rivers. He had seen the well-dressed men

and women of all colors standing on the decks.

Kline had been very young when he and Isaac Bell had been in New Orleans, but his memory was good. After he learned to walk and talk as the White-eyes did, he would make his way to Mexico, and if he liked, he would live life there. For a long time, he had not been able to get the whisky that had ruled his life. Unknowingly, that had worked in his favor. These last few months, he had been able to cast off its hold on him. He was wise enough to know he must stay away from the strong drink, for it impaired him and made him crazy. Now he would see what it was like to live the life of the free man.

For the next few weeks, he traveled only at night. He began to see many settlements and sometimes large cities along the river. Once, he slept in an empty barn loft and watched the people walk along the streets of a town the following day. People, both Black and White, moved about and seemed not to notice one another. If he dressed in clothing as he saw below him, he could walk the streets and not be detected. Lying in the hayloft, he removed his headband. He decided to try out his theory in this town. The ringing of a hammer along the street got his attention. At the end of the street, he noticed the blacksmith was a Black man just as large as he was. Jo waited for nightfall and then climbed from the loft. Standing in the shadows he watched the blacksmith's shop.

As evening approached, the town settled down, and there was little movement along that end of the street. Jo made his way behind the blacksmith's shop to the small house where he had seen the blacksmith go. Through the window, Kline watched the Black man preparing food. The blacksmith was alone. Jo waited until the man sat down to eat the food he had prepared. Then the man did a strange thing, he bowed his head and with his hands clasped together and his eyes closed he talked out loud. This was the time Jo walked in and stood against the closed door. The man stood and, for a few awkward moments, the two looked at one another. Jo had been practicing a phrase that he thought would be best to say. "I need your help," Kline stated. The puzzled look of the man indicated he did not understand. The clothing Bald Jo Kline had changed into did not fit well. His mannerism and speech were that of an Indian. Jo continued to repeat the phrase. Finally, the man's face lit up, and he understood. Fear turned to curiosity with that understanding. "You need my help?" Earl the blacksmith exclaimed.

To the blacksmith, it was evident that the man standing before him had been living with the Indians for a long time. Kline was relieved, and it was a given that the man did not know of Bald Jo Kline or Black Hawk. Attempts to communicate were made back and forth.

Days turned into weeks as the blacksmith taught Jo to speak. Bald Jo Kline never spoke a word when people came around and Earl, the blacksmith, explained that he was a mute. Every night, he showed Jo the words in a big black book and had him speak the words until he could say them. Each night he would read from the book and pray for the food they were about to eat. The days in the blacksmith shop were spent teaching Jo how to shoe horses and care for them. Jo learned to repair wagon wheels. People came and went at which time Jo would always stay in the back working on something, but always listening to the conversation between the blacksmith and the customer.

Then came the Sunday that Earl laid out two suits of clothes and explained that they would be going to a camp meeting down by the river. Neither Jo nor Earl had shoes because their feet were very big and shoes were hard to come by. After a good bath in a stream back of the blacksmith's home, the two dressed and walked through the town. They passed a white building with a wooden cross and Earl hummed the tune the people in the building were singing.

The camp meeting was held a little further down along a river that was flowing fast from a recent rain. The river was fierce with logs and debris churning in the cold water. They came to a place where wagons and mules were tied to trees and a large gathering of Black people were already singing songs and clapping their hands. Jo was beginning to get comfortable with his new life. It brought a new feeling of freedom to him. After the service, families sat around on blankets and had a meal. A woman from each family had prepared and brought in baskets of food.

Upon the bluff the church had turned out and folks were leaving, headed home. Jo and Earl started back along the road after eating with a family that had brought a large basket. Suddenly a woman screamed, and a wagon pulled by two horses bolted through the crowd headed straight for the river. Dogs took in after the running horses which made the horses run wild. Situations like this were nothing new to the Black Hawk. He had stayed alive by knowing what to do in the worst of situations. He saw the horses bolt over a cliff and a woman and small child were thrown into the raging river. Instantly, he was on his feet running toward the river. The woman had been rescued quickly, but the child was instantly taken far from the bank. The small head bobbed up and down in the fast-moving water. Jo ran through the crowd of people. Men were down running along the river, but none were trying to swim out to the child. Bald Jo Kline was back in his element. Running above them on the cliff, he kept his eyes on the bobbing red head and small white hands thrashing in the river. The river came to a turn where the cliff jutted out close to the water. Taking sail, Jo flew out over the water like the mighty fearless warrior he had been in the past. He came up far down the river fighting to keep his head above water and locate the small child. As if by Divine Providence a small hand grabbed Jo by the collar of his coat and Jo quickly lifted her up where she could breathe.

The bank had been searched for miles and just before dark it was called off and men both Black and White made their way back to the church where a sad quiet had fallen over the people. The quietness was punctuated by the moans and cries of the mother and father who had lost their first born.

That night the stars came out and a clear sky made a canopy over the small church and all the mourners surrounding it. By the light from the windows men walked about speaking of the brave way the tall Black man had died trying to save Cap and Lindsey Franks only child. No one noticed Bald Jo Kline walking up through the milling crowd and enter the little church. Inside the sanctuary Lindsey Franks had just stood and turned. The child laying asleep on Jo's shoulder suddenly woke and turned to see her mother. Jo stooped down on one knee and let the child run to her startled mother.

Bald Jo did not understand this next gesture. Every man and woman surrounded him and either shook his hand or patted him on his back. Earl quickly got Jo away from the crowd and the two walked home in the dark, leaving an overflowing church singing hymns. All was well that night in River Dale.

The next morning a smiling group of men came to the blacksmith shop where Jo and Earl were repairing a broken wagon wheel. The men had Jo sit down and they drew Jo's feet out on pieces of leather. A lone rider appeared and, taking the leather pieces, rode off down the road. The two looked at each other questioning what was going on but soon dismissed it and went back to work.

On a cool and windy morning a week later, the same men asked the two to come to the little church. Getting Jo to sit down they produced two pairs of leather boots. They were the best and latest styles and Jo's feet slid easily into the first pair. Jo looked at the second pair and quickly made Earl sit and he got down on his knees and placed them on Earl's feet. All in the church clapped and patted the two men on the back.

The attention Jo was receiving was too much and a week later he decided to continue his trip to New Orleans. He knew now he could make the transition to his new way of life.

One night while eating supper together, Jo spoke to his new friend of his plans to leave. Earl was devastated but agreed to help Jo get his poke together. In this time of civilized life with Earl, he had relearned how to hold a spoon and fork and eat properly at a table. Jo Kline never forgot how to understand English but had lost his ability to speak English. The words would not come out right. Speaking English was his biggest problem. It was a slow process, but he was determined. In a few weeks he had been able to start picking up the pronunciations. Each day the blacksmith had taken Jo for strolls down the main street, usually at the time of day when the streets were empty. Jo realized there had been a profound change in the way people lived over the twenty years since he had left civilization. He realized that if he stuck to the Black community while he was in the learning stage, he would be able to make the transition with little effort.

A week later, the blacksmith helped him buy a horse. Jo was inclined just to steal a horse but watching the blacksmith haggle over the price of the horse greatly interested him. Now feeling secure on land, he no longer needed the canoe, and before he shoved it out in the fast-moving river, he slashed the bottom.

As he and the blacksmith rode through town one rainy evening, Jo was surprised to see a man hanging from gallows in the town square. "What says the sign?" Jo asked the blacksmith regarding the sign around the dead man's neck.

"Horse Thief," the blacksmith said.

Jo asked Earl about the laws and he showed Kline the ten commandments in the black book. Earl explained to him that these laws were the backbone of all laws. Now Kline realized he had to live by the White man's laws.

Months passed while Jo Kline acclimated to the new world, he was living in. He had learned all he needed to know about horses, so he decided it was time to leave.

"Take this book. It will help you learn to speak the English language with eloquence. Being able to talk well will bring you respect from a great many folks," said Earl.

Getting final instructions on his trip south, Jo headed for New Orleans. On his way south, he passed through many towns. There were many sights to see. In a store window, he saw books and he purchased some. Earl had told him to read to himself out loud each day, pronouncing the words slowly. This one thing quickened his education and gave him confidence.

An old memory passed through his mind as he thought of the lovely woman he had taken years before. She had a little book just like the one Earl had given him. She had clung to it in her frightened state. This book had the same writing on its cover.

The shocking memory of meeting his son was part of that same memory and gave him reason to end the Indian way of life. In his son, he saw a man he could have become if he had wanted to. He had many sons, but this one was different. He had a spirit that set him apart from the others.

Many days later, he reached the city of New Orleans. It was an amazing place, and he wandered along the streets freely, listening to the talk and looking at the wares the street merchants displayed. From this city, if he headed northwest, it could take him back where the Comanche and Apache Indians still raided the southern plains. For just a moment, he was tempted to become the feared warrior with young pallatons at his beckon call. Bald Jo also knew the Bluecoats were on every street corner. His name was well known here, and he would have to be careful. Jo spotted several Black women walking ahead of him and decided to follow along. Getting down from his horse, he became less noticeable as he made his way along the street.

C08 - The Wages of Sin

Far North of Bald Jo Kline, Jericho Dawson leaned forward and strained to see in the darkness. "I don't see any movement down there," he said. "You stay up here, Pike, and cover me. I'll go down and see if there's Indians still around." Jericho eased back from the tree line where the wagon sat and quickly disappeared into the tree-covered terrain. Jericho moved around the burned-out trading post and waved an all-clear to Cleve and Pike seated on the wagon seat. Moments later, the three walked slowly around the burned-out building.

The trading post sat on the edge of a large river among the low hills. Pike's trading post had been a scenic place. It had been well-constructed and built to defend against Indian attacks. Each window had been fitted with heavy wood shutters with small ports to shoot from. A quick survey of the structure indicated the force of the blast when the powder kegs had been set off. The roof still smoldered even after a hard rain had put the fire out. Embers swirled up from the heat and smoldering logs.

Pike walked around the building and sighed because this had been his business as well as his home. For a long time, the three stood looking at the blackened structure. They talked low, not wanting their voices to carry in the early morning breeze.

"Jericho, from the smell of rotting flesh, I would say there is a lot of Indians squashed under that roof. The only way to get to the furs is through the tunnel. The herd should get here around noon. We need to have as many furs out as possible, ready for the squaws to make clothing. It is turning mighty cold," Pike said.

"So, you say! Let's get to it!" Jericho said.

Crawling back through the tunnel gave them an eerie feeling. With candles, they saw the cellar had been secure and sealed from the water.

"Cleve, you are the smallest. You stay down here with me and start dragging the furs and boxes to the end of the tunnel. Jericho will be above at the opening and carry the goods to the wagon," Pike said.

The work went on for hours, and there were goods that Pike had forgotten he had. One such find was several boxes of jeans and three boxes of flannel shirts. This would transform the Indians from the tribe to dark-skinned children in overalls.

ααααααα

Christian and Patrick led Joe Bess and the women along a wilderness trail back along a mountainside. The canyon walls cast dark shadows above them as they picked their way through the boulders and trees. Gathering rainclouds soon blanketed the sky in darkness. Then the rain came, heavy and cold. Long past midnight, they stumbled along in the dark. Occasionally, they found themselves in a stream of knee-deep rushing water.

"Patrick, how much further? We need to find shelter and get out of this cold rain. The temperature is dropping fast," Christian said.

"Shelter is just ahead," Patrick stated.

A few minutes later, they walked under an overhang that afforded them a dry place against a mountainside. Below Patrick's mountainside refuge, it was high and dry. Water running off the mountain gave them the appearance of being behind a waterfall.

Patrick lit a lantern and smiled at the woodpile he had left the night he had seen the raft in the river. His furs were all intact, and his mule was still in the small meadow behind his mountainside cave. Handing Joe Bess and the girls a dry blanket, he said, "I just wish the kids were here now. We will rest for the remaining hours before the first light. By noon if the weather clears, we should be at the homestead of my brother. I just hope that William and Running Deer beat us there," Patrick said.

Several miles away in the moonlit night, the wind and rain moved on, and the moon occasionally appeared. William jerked awake and, moving his foot, touched Running Deer's foot. He could see her face in the pale moonlight, and without moving, her eyes opened and instantly had a look of awareness. The two had chosen their bed spot against the boulders that afforded protection from behind. There was only one direction an attack could come, but that left only one way to escape as well. Running Deer had chosen well out of the wind and rain.

William eased Miller's rifle into position and eased the safety off. Squinting his eyes, he watched the darkness. Hours of rain and wind eased their fears, and they relaxed—both snug and warm in the heavy buffalo robe.

"I believe that Black Hawk is no longer following us. He will be seeking shelter from this cold weather. Now we need to decide where we are going. There is a fort along the river, but to get there, we would surely see more Indians," Running Deer said.

"Have you ever been to the river the trappers call the Sandy Wash?" William asked.

"Yes, it would be behind this mountain and away from the big river. My father used to trap along it when I was younger. When I was little, my family and I canoed the Sandy Wash many times," Running Deer said.

"My home is a mile from the Wishbone upstream on Sandy Wash. That is where we need to go. Once we are there, we will be safe," William said. The bad memories came flooding back to him, but he put them out of his mind. He was finally able to deal with the grief and loss.

William remembered the leather clothing they wore and spoke. "Running Deer, if all is well at my home, tomorrow we will change into clothes my mother made. We will no longer be considered Indians. My English is coming back. We will always remember what we have been through, making us strong," William said.

C09 – Memories

F ar ahead, the home of Clayton and
Etta Murphy stood barren and
neglected. Patrick was delighted the
cellar still held Etta's can goods. It seemed
ages since Patrick had been there, and the
sad memories were hard to deal with. He
had to keep reminding himself of the great
hope that Christians have. *'Though we are not
exempt from the tragedies of this world, we the
people of the Bible have hope. I know I will see
Etta and Clayton again. Of this, I am certain,'*
he reasoned. This hope helped him deal
with the grief and gave him hope of seeing
William alive, knowing God would bring
the lad home safely.

Outside, the little Ginny brayed and
lifted her nose to the wind blowing hard
out of the north. Something was a-comin'
for sure. This Patrick could tell from her
attitude. Making up a perimeter of defense,
Patrick, Christian, and Joe Bess watched
the long prairie that bordered the west side
of the Sandy Wash.

"Something or someone is coming.
The mule knows," Patrick stated. A short
time later three men on horses and walking
behind them several mountain men
carrying packs appeared.

They were obviously forward scouts
for what was making the dust cloud. The

wind brought the sound of cattle bawling a mile or so behind the men.

"Patrick, if I'm not mistaken, there is a cattle drive headed this way with an odd mixture of people. Following behind a rough-looking bunch of men all wrapped in buffalo robes," Joe Bess said.

Far back along the river, the tribe came following the rough mountain men. Behind the tribe came a mule-drawn wagon and a rough-looking old steer leading a herd of fine cattle.

Patrick laughed and handed the field glass to Joe Bess. "I think I've seen it all now," Patrick said, not knowing exactly how to explain what he was seeing.

Joe Bess scanned the forward group of mountain men through the field glass. Far up the river, a dust cloud filled the air as a cold wind blew straight south ahead of the herd. There was something familiar about one of the horses and rider ahead of the herd. This man was wrapped in a buffalo robe, but it was Indian clothes that this man was wearing. "Well, have either of you ever seen an Indian cattle drive?" Joe asked. Questioning looks came from Patrick and Christian.

"That is the only way I can explain what is coming. There is a tribe of Indians dressed in overalls and buffalo robes," Joe stated.

The herd came through a field of corn long since neglected. They scattered and started eating the old ears of corn, brown stalks, and remnants of a lost crop. That stopped the forward progress and the Indians. Wanting to be out of the cold wind, they began setting up camp next to the Sandy Wash.

Patrick and Christian recognized Jericho Dawson and went across the open ground to greet him. They were hoping to learn if William and Running Deer were among those coming.

Hank Lightfoot let his horse go and quickly started supervising the tribe setting camp for a cold night.

"June, I think I know that horse," Joe said. Taking up his walking cane, he started moving over to the horse. It was not long until recognition settled on his face. It was the mare he had given to Hank when they parted after the war. A young black stud colt moved around the mare, and Joe Bess saw the exact image of his horse Dancer in the young colt. Then he recognized Hank's mother and father among the tribe setting up camp. Then came the moment of assurance. Next to the Sandy Wash, a tall Indian was setting up his old red tent. Joe's eyes watered, and he stood leaning on his crutch, taking a moment to get hold of his emotions.

Walking up behind Hank he said, "That is a mighty odd tent. I had one like that once."

Recognizing Joe's voice, Hank turned and the two clasped hands. Both had a hard time with their emotions for a few minutes.

Patrick was sad that William was not among the group but was encouraged to know that he had been seen. While Patrick and Christian made plans to head back into the wilderness to look for the children, two specks made their way along the wash. Patrick was the first to recognize the proud way William had always walked. Then it became a foot race as the two were able to identify their kin standing in front of the cabin. Months of sadness were shed like a winter coat of gloom. Patrick instantly realized that young William had become a man. A man after God's own heart. William had been tested by fire and found to be approved.

A week later, a smiling group of people sat around the cabin table. It was a thanksgiving for all that cold morning. Everyone eyed the wild turkey Patrick had shot. Christian spoke first about the plans he and Running Deer (Leah) had. The clothes of William's mother and father had transformed their appearance. They were now ready to enter the White world and make their way to her grandfather's home in Virginia. There they would decide where their life would take them.

"William, will you come with us? I cannot imagine leaving you behind," Running Deer pleaded.

William looked at Patrick, and the two smiled at each other. "Leah, I guess we need to call you Leah. I could not keep William here. He wants to be with you, and he needs to be away for a while. Maybe going to school back east would help you two re-adjust. You two can make your plans according to what you decide is best for you. I am home! My rambling days are over," Patrick said.

Joe Bess looked at the people sitting around the table and directed his words to Sarah and June. "You two need to make a choice. You can take the barge ride, and in a few days be in New Orleans. Sarah, it has been a long haul, and you have come through it a better and stronger person. The herd will be back on the trail again in a few days. I will leave with the herd for the hill country of Texas. June, I hope you and Sarah will come with me. A trail drive, this time of year will be hard, but you two have seen much worse. You can take the quick way to New Orleans and be back in civilization in just a few days or come with me. It will take a month or more to get home, but if you come, you will have a home when we arrive there," Joe Bess said.

June looked at Joe, and her countenance dropped. She tried to talk but just turned and walked out of the house.

That night she sat and, by lantern light, poured out her heart on a piece of paper. That morning Joe came in from talking with the drovers to find a letter propped up on the table with his name on it.

Patrick had hailed a barge captain and sold his furs. "The captain will get us to Mount Pleasant, and from there, a sternwheeler will get us to New Orleans," June said. That next morning before the fog lifted, the heavily loaded barge made its way past the Wishbone. All was quiet as the men on the poles removed their hats and held them over their hearts giving their respect as they recalled the massacre. Sarah breathed a sigh of relief for soon they would be in civilization. They had left early, and June stood solemnly, watching the river carry them along.

C10 - Broken Past

It wasn't unusual to hear a steam whistle blowing on the Mississippi. Big paddle wheelers ferried people across the Mississippi and out along the Gulf of Mexico. They were loaded with bales of cotton and assorted military and farming needs. The war had long since ended, and New Orleans was busting at the seams. Things were slowly getting back to a new normal—a normal where anything that would bring a buck was considered. Corruption had reached a new high.

Jo Kline now went by the name of Henry Jackson. He had grown accustomed to the activity he saw along the street. He loved the nightlife and openly engaged in conversation with anyone on the street. Jo had no problem with the transition from the Indian dialect to English. His English pronunciations had an interesting Spanish flavor from a youth he thought he had forgotten. Mixing with the many different Blacks from the islands and South America made his English and new identity believable. He had been able to understand buying and selling quickly. Dealing in currency and making the correct change made his mind sharpen much quicker.

It was April. Jo Kline considered how cold it would have been out on the high prairie and along the upper Arkansas and Missouri rivers the past few months. The winter had been mild here in New Orleans, and now flowers were in bloom, and spring was in the air. This warm spring morning, Jo Kline made his way along the crowded streets. On every street in the French Quarter, street vendors hawked their wares—everything from paintings and jewelry to clothing.

During the weeks Kline had spent in New Orleans, he had learned the mannerisms of the local gentry and how to eat correctly. All due to a person by the name of Big Hattie Jackson. Big Hattie as she was called, came walking along the riverfront, dressed for show and with an impressive entourage. Beside her, a well-dressed man in a green tuxedo and top hat carried a silk parasol to keep the bright sun off Hattie's ebony face. She was a bit plump but a natural beauty and had taken a liking to Jo Kline at first glance. It did not take long until she had started taking the rough edges off his demeanor. Under her wing, she taught him all the basics of being a gentleman. He now walked swinging a silver-studded cane, as did most gentlemen of means in New Orleans. The cane was a clever weapon that hid within its length a sword as sharp as a razor and in his hands as deadly as a rattlesnake. Under his tailored coat were the latest pistols. One thing Bald Jo Kline had not given up was keeping as many of the best weapons he could get always on his person.

Jo was a quick learner. He had become skillful at buying and selling quality horses. Should anyone inquire, he was a horse buyer traveling the lower southern states looking for good breeding and riding stock for his ranch in Mexico. He knew there was money to be made selling horses to the military on both sides of the border.

Jo was a head taller than most folks which made it easy to get around the streets of New Orleans. A well-dressed gentleman standing ahead of Jo blocked his sight, and Jo heard a voice say.

"Dr. Lacy, your passage aboard the Mississippi Queen for Galveston has been confirmed. You and your wife will have a stateroom, and boarding will start at 7 am," the ticket master said as he handed the well-dressed man his tickets.

Jo Kline had been standing right behind Dr. Horace Lacy. He was shocked. Even though he had never seen Horace Lacy, he knew the name. The name was in the little book the woman he loved had carried in her pocket. Daily she prayed and repeated the man's name. He also knew that his son bore the Lacy name. As Dr. Lacy turned, the two came face to face.

"Pardon me," Dr. Lacy said as he stepped around Bald Jo. As Dr. Lacy walked away, Jo quickly looked around to see if the woman he had taken so many years ago was with this man. Jo Kline had not realized it, but he had been standing in the ticket line for the Mississippi River Queen, a steam-powered paddle wheeler.

His concentration was broken as a voice behind him said. "Sir, are you purchasing a ticket? You are holding up the line," the ticket master said.

Jo instantly turned back to the counter and stared at the Ticket Master for a minute. He was perplexed as to whether he would buy a ticket or not. On the spur of the moment, he said, "Yes, I will need a stateroom, and I have three horses."

A blast from a riverboat whistle silenced all conversation along the dock as the great Mississippi River Queen made the dock from Baton Rouge. The trip downriver for the Queen had been perfect as the river was running swift and little coal had been consumed in the steam boilers.

Everyone stopped what they were doing to watch the big ship dock. People lined the deck railings of the majestic paddle-wheeler waving to friends along the dock. One single individual stood on the top deck and watched as the gangplank was lowered. The man handing a silver coin to the purser that stood next to the rail and said, "Mr. Wineseal, would you please make sure my mules and dogs are fed and watered while we are in port. I will be in New Orleans to visit the home of Dr.

Horace Lacy until the Queen leaves on the morrow," Jonathan Masters said.

"Rest assured, Professor Masters, I will make them my highest priority," Wineseal said. Wineseal wondered about the solemn man that never took his top hat off. Obviously, from the scars that gave his left ear and forehead an odd angle, this man had been cut badly. It appeared he might have been scalped and lived to talk about it.

Jonathan Masters saw the man he was looking for below him on the dock and, after waving to Horace Lacy, made his way to the lower deck.

The whistle finally finished its loud and overpowering blast, and the ticket agent finished talking to the tall Black gentlemen standing before him. "Your ticket will cost you four dollars for the stateroom, and the horses will be stalled below deck. Have them here early to board. They will cost you two bits apiece extra. The river Queen will start boarding at 7 a.m.," the Ticket Master said.

Pocketing the ticket, Jo Kline stepped away from the line and scanned the people along the wharf. Walking over to the river, he watched the activity. The hustle and bustle in the White man's world were completely different from his life as an Indian. Now it was time to move along. Things did not feel right. Bald Jo Kline had become restless. He pulled the expensive gold watch from his watch pocket and flipped open the cover. This watch had been his good-luck piece. When they had attacked a wagon train, a warrior had stepped up from behind him and taken a bullet meant for him. He had found the watch with the gold chain in a dead woman's pocket below the warrior who had saved his life.

The watch had been in the chest all these years until Big Hattie had dressed him in the finest suit. Once in New Orleans, he had noticed all the gentlemen who walked New Orleans' streets had a gold watch and chain. It had prompted him to go to the chest. There in a black velvet sack was the watch. It reminded him of the one great love of his life. Suddenly a chilly breeze touched the back of his neck, and it caused goosebumps along his spine. Something told him it was time to leave New Orleans. Smiling, he felt a surge of pride in himself. It had been the power over the weak-minded warriors that had fed his ego in the past. Now he could function in the White man's world as efficiently as in the Indian lands. This time the power was over intelligent men—this time, it was different.

That night he packed his brass-trimmed chest Big Hattie had given him. The next morning he blended in with the other well-dressed men as he traveled down the mighty Mississippi and out in the

Gulf. It would take several days crossing the Gulf to reach Corpus Christi on the Texas coast. He would be back in the land where the name Bald Jo Kline and Black Hawk struck fear in people's hearts. He would buy horses adding to his string, and head for Mexico this time. There he would once again live as a Mexican don. He could dress like an Indian, become Black Hawk again, and make raids along the border stealing horses. The future held purpose. It was much better now than just a few months ago when the cavalry hunted him.

On the Mississippi Queen, he would follow the woman he had so loved from a distance. He knew this was not wise, but he wanted to see her. Jo was not sure what would happen if she recognized him. He had two cravings— one was the woman, and the other was the spirit in the bottle. Either one would someday get him killed if he were not careful.

Knowing it would be dangerous, he locked all his belongings in the big chest, except the things he needed daily he kept in a large carpet bag. He would have the chest shipped to himself in Corpus Christi. If he had to get away quickly, he would have the money and clothes to restart his life again. It was getting late. He needed to rest and read from the book. The book was touching a part of him he did not know he had. Bald Jo knew no fear, but his new life required him to change his way of living and become like the civilized men. Being or acting civilized was the hard part for Bald Jo Kline, for he loved the fear he could put in people.

That night Dr. Horace Lacy and his friend Jonathan Masters sat across the table from each other. Other than the correspondence, this was the first face-to-face meeting since their college days. Rising from his seat, Horace approached his friend on the other end of the table.

"Jonathan, while we talk, the doctor in me wants to have a look at the damage to your scalp. I think I can relieve some of the skin tightness on the left side of your face. That will make your eyelid set back in place, and your appearance with a hat on will be normal. There is a doctor named Black that could do much more for you than I can. He is no longer here in New Orleans," Horace stated.

"Anything you can do will be an improvement," Jonathan said in a jovial manner. His heart and mind were in turmoil despite his controlled appearance.

While Dr. Lacy looked at the tightness and scars on Jonathan's head, Jonathan turned his attention to Samantha Lacy.

"Samantha, I know this will be hard for you, but I need to know all you can tell me of the last moments of Elizabeth's life on that fateful day when I left with the mules headed across the prairie. The last time I looked back, you were walking with Elizabeth. We were unwise to take the Snow wagon train west. We were pilgrims shepherded by a fool. Billy Snow knew nothing of what was coming. The Indian that attacked me jumped me at the river, and even though I drowned him, he did this to me. I know it will be painful for you, but I need to know the story. I want to know of my wife's last moments of life," Jonathan asked.

Samantha Lacy stood and walked across the room. Standing by the window, she crossed her arms and fastened her gaze on the people that passed in the street.

"Jonathan, we were babes in the wilderness. Totally unaware of what evil lurked in this beautiful land. It was a hot day—your birthday, I recall. Elizabeth and I were laughing together. She had brought a present for you all the way from back east. She was waiting for the right time to give it to you. I asked her what birthday present could she have possibly brought you from back East that would be useful in the wilderness. She had it in her pocket but never got a chance to show it to me or answer my question. One moment we were laughing; the next, she lay dead with an arrow sticking in her heart. One moment we were happy and excited about the good life we planned in the new world. Then there was no future. Our dreams and plans all perished, tumbling down in a hideous moment of time, never to be the same again," Samantha said.

Jonathan thought for a moment. Clearing his throat, he said. "In the past eighteen years of nineteen now, I have roamed the wide expanses of the prairie. I have fought Indians, hoping to kill or be killed, looking for the evil one that destroyed my world. Several times I came close. I realized the hate I harbored was beginning to eat me—body and soul. I had lost all compassion for anyone. My deadly skills improved. Over the years, I became dangerous with any weapon in my hands. I became a bounty hunter and brought many a man to justice. Very seldom did I bring them in alive. I hunted men like animals— the fiercer the men or mountain lion, the better. I had a death wish. It came to me that Kline was recently killed in a battle. Whether it is true or not, my way of life is set. The war has made many bad men, and they must be stopped. The Indians on the plains need to hear the gospel. So, I ride hunting men or beasts and preaching to all who will hear me. I am called the Wilderness Preacher or a modern-day John the Baptist by many who know me in the hills. Now I want to put to rest the questions I have and live for the day I can join Elizabeth. If I find that Kline is still alive, I will follow him to hell to stop his evil. My second reason for coming was to see my good friends and have a pleasantly uneventful trip with you two on a sternwheeler. In Baton Rouge, I picked up some Bloodhound pups to train for tracking lawless men. I see no other use for my life than fighting the evil that dominates this fair land. I have resolved to live like that," he said.

αααααααα

It was the last day of January when General Lew Wallace took his seat behind the courtroom bench and called the court to order. The general had been making his way to New Mexico when his travels brought him to La Fuego in the hill country of Texas. The war left a deep and bitter rift in the small community. The General felt obligated to make every effort to quell some of the town's hurt and bitterness. So, he deployed his troops to help the local sheriff maintain order. The first thing that had to be done was help remove the rowdy drunks. He was obliged to take charge of the civil or uncivil proceedings in La Fuego. After gathering all the information about crimes committed during the war against civilians, the General had his troops erect a very-high-gallows on the main street at the very door of the courthouse.

General Lew Wallace was a lawyer and Union General in the Civil War. Since the war's end, he had unsuccessfully run for congress. His passion was writing, and he was working on a novel called Ben Hur. His travels were a means of gathering new ideas for new books from the culture he was exposed to.

His notoriety did not seem to impress the locals. So, as was his custom in his day-to-day affairs, he relied on divine leadership, praying for the wisdom of Solomon in all situations he found himself. He hoped to convince the town to come together and dispense with the bitterness and hate the war had left.

The gallows looked odd in the street, but he wanted to bring reality to the townspeople. Hate bred hate and killing had to be dealt with by the law. Death and eternity were real, and the townspeople needed to change their attitudes to a forgiving outlook. This town was not far from having a clan-like war in the streets.

The local cowboys did not help the tense situations. There was a handful of drunks in the local jail, more being added daily. Upon arrival, Lew made a new ruling. The only way cowboys from the local ranches could get out of jail was to leave town and not return for at least six months. That was after their ranch boss came in person and paid their fines.

The town needed a breather from all this craziness. The sheriff had his hands full because he was the main target of this hatred. Accusations flew back and forth with no proof. Lew figured this hearing would furnish him with plenty of stories for a new novel. Having a genuine Yankee General presiding should depolarize the town folks.

On a Monday morning, dressed in his best uniform, the general took his seat in a packed courtroom and called the proceedings to order.

A local spokesperson stood before the courtroom and called for the first person to speak on these matters. The appointed speaker was Dr. Ben Turner who had been chosen by the General. Ben called out loud and clear.

"At this time, the General asks Sheriff Walter Stevens to testify concerning the events that occurred over the years of the Civil War," Ben said.

There was a loud murmuring from the town folks that had assembled, and scuffling broke out. It took the butts of the soldier's rifles to bring the courtroom back to order.

"Sergeant Kimble, take those men to the jail and lock them up," the general said.

That intolerant response put a sudden damper on anyone who wanted to get loud because the jail was full. Obviously, some in the courtroom favored hanging a bunch of people they hated. On seeing the gallows, the town folk showed up to see who would swing. A few were in favor of just running the Yankee General out of town and starting the civil war all over again.

Sheriff Stevens stood and made his way to the front of the courtroom, where a woman met him with a large Bible and a pair of spectacles clinging to her nose.

A deadly quiet fell over the courtroom as no one had heard Sheriff Stevens speak and doubted he had anything to say but lies to cover up his crimes. He would surely swing.

With his hands on the Holy Bible, the sheriff was sworn in. His eyes were locked with Ben Turner's as he said, "I do." No one knew what had transpired in this man's heart. Ben Turner knew the papers in the sheriffs' hands were true. The sheriff stood in the witness chair and read aloud—one by one—all the atrocities that had occurred over the years of war. In reality, it was soon disclosed that almost all the evil done by the night riders could be laid at the feet of four men—Fred Bates, Pate Ledbetter, and his two gunmen, Stone and Barber. The sheriff did not believe Ledbetter was Pate's real name. Without exception, all the men mentioned were dead. That left those night riders that were not mentioned and the damage to property, barns, and homes to deal with.

In most cases, the men who torched the barns had been shot dead on the spot. A dynamite blast permanently blinded one and disfigured three more. So, there was little that could be done to them. They would suffer enough for their crimes for the rest of their lives.

Then came the witnesses, one by one, that told of loved ones that died in the war. Young men cut down in their youth. Parents that couldn't cope and committed suicide. Young fathers that would never return. The grief that poured out in the courtroom was overwhelming.

The one great loss that could have brought the people together was the day Doc Ben Turner (God's man in the pulpit) was dismissed. The very man the town needed because of his medical and spiritual insight had been removed from fellowship at a time of their greatest need. That day the fellowship the church needed fell apart. That one place that could have been used for healing, lay barren and deserted for the rest of the war. Had the fellowship of believers been left in tact, there would have been a Balm-in-Gilead. A solace to ease the pain of grief and suffering had the people of God stayed together; had they yielded to the leadership of God Almighty rather than choosing sides for war. If this town would have gathered behind the cross, believing God's loving care would get them through the war years, things would have turned out differently.

Some of the townspeople had come to see a hanging or two. They did not have the capacity and did not want to hear this forgiveness stuff. They quietly eased out of the courthouse, still bitter and unsatisfied.

The grudges and hate harbored by neighbors on this January day melted away. But for the people of God that made up much of the community, there was a great working of the Holy Spirit right there in the courthouse, and God heard from Heaven and healed their land.

Tapping his gavel, the general cleared his throat and said, "I turn this healing process over to the godly men and women who will work to get La Fuego back on its feet. God Bless your efforts and give you the wisdom to withstand the devil's own. Now, what is to be done with the gallows setting outside?" he asked.

The answer came from the back of the courtroom, "Long live the Confederacy! Hang yourself! You Yankee Carpetbagger!"

"This court is adjourned," replied Lew Wallace shaking his head.

Needless to say, no one was hung that day, and Sheriff Walter Stevens received for his genuine repentance a chance to walk upright. Years later, he died saving a child from a burning building. He had become and was remembered as the most respected and loved Sheriff La Fuego, Texas, ever had. *'My—my, what God can do with so little to work with!'*

αααααααα

On a cold February day, a stagecoach pulled up to the entrance of a long valley in the hill country. While the team of horses took a blow, the teamster riding shotgun said, "Jake, I see a smoking chimney over the trees. This must be the place. Take us on down the valley."

It had been a grueling ride for two of the occupants of the stagecoach. However, it had been much better than waking each morning on the cold ground downwind of a prairie full of cattle lowing. It was disheartening to say the least. The ride from New Orleans had been mostly by train, but this last part of the journey had been by coach and had ended just east of a long valley that had turned brown with the cold winter months.

A stagecoach coming down their valley was a first for Ben Turner and Pete Cooper. Pete walked from the barn carrying a pail of milk. Ben Turner and Reddy Bell stepped from the house to watch the stagecoach coming down the dusty road. After the dust had settled, the driver jumped down and opened the stagecoach door. Down from the coach first stepped June and then Sarah Walsh. June looked the two men over before saying to the man with the pail. "You must be Pete Cooper, and you must be Dr. Ben Turner. We have come a long way to meet you. My name is June Walsh, and this is my sister Sarah. That young man must be Reddy Bell. I feel I know you three already. I have heard so much about you," she said.

Reddy did not acknowledge the pretty lady speaking. Instead, he had already spotted Sarah. The two stood grinning at each other.

June noticed the youthful smiles being passed between the two and raised her eyebrow before saying, "Joe Bess sends his love and has sent Sarah and me on ahead to alert you of what you will see coming down this valley shortly. Not only is Joe coming with a group of punchers pushing a large herd, but Hank Lightfoot and his family are also leading an entire tribe of Indians. Sarah and I did not particularly want to sleep on the cold ground with a bunch of smelly drovers, so we came ahead to make ready for the wedding!" June said.

C11 - The Second Fiddle Man

In New Orleans, a steady downpour hampered the loading of passengers on the Mississippi Queen. Bald Jo Kline had come early and checked his chest with the ticket agent. Making his way across the animal loading platform, he followed a deckhand leading his mares while he led the prize stud. He had learned a lot about horses, and a stallion will always follow a mare obediently.

Moving down the ramp, he turned his head to scan the arrivals on the dock. His heart skipped a beat. There she was older, more mature, but more beautiful than she had been so many years ago. She stood between two men, the doctor he had seen face-to-face—the other man as tall as he but had an odd look from this distance. Jo Kline stood between the two horses, covered with a raincoat and hat. They shielded him from being identifiable. From now on, he would always wear a hat or dress in a manner as to cover most of his face when he was not in his stateroom. He must not move about openly because he had immediately identified the woman even after all these years. No doubt she could do the same. He had dressed in Spanish riding gear and donned a New Orleans style hat on this day.

The crewman forked fresh hay into the stall and patted the neck of the mare. "These are fine horses! You know good horseflesh!" he said.

Jo Kline bent down and petted some puppies in a cage clamoring for his attention and nodded a yes in response. "I only buy large, strong horses that can carry a man my size like that big mule over there. Most people don't like riding a mule, but they are strong and can carry a heavy load all day. These are fine dogs! They have good breeding," he added.

"They belong to a gentleman that boarded in Baton Rouge. His name is Masters over from Texas. He came all the way to Baton Rouge to purchase these fine Bloodhounds. I think he must have been scalped long ago from looking at the scars on the side of his head. My name is Wineseal. I will be caring for your horses. They will be well cared for, I assure you," Wineseal stated.

Kline contemplated what the man had said before taking a silver coin out of his pocket and giving it to the crewman. "Make sure that you do. I always want the halter and lead ropes on them. I have a Spanish saddle I will bring down for you to clean and oil," Jo said.

"Very good, sir," Wineseal stated. "As you wish, it shall be done."

Looking around at the animal boarding platform, Bald Jo noticed how it was held in place. Making mental notes, he moved to the stairs that led to the upper decks.

Pulling his hat down, he stepped out onto the main deck in a heavy downpour. His stateroom was on the second deck, and it was only a short walk to the stairs. The rain blew against his slicker as he walked along the deck, noting the numbers on the doors.

His saddle and riding gear, weapons, and the carpetbag had all been delivered to his room—one door from the outside and one into the hall. Hattie Jackson's initials (HJ) were on the carpetbag. Jo had been using the name Henry Jackson since he had met Big Hattie and acquired the big chest and bag with her initials on them.

There were several days of traveling before the coast of Texas appeared. Kline spent the daylight hours in his room or down where the horses were stabled. His meals were delivered by Wineseal personally and always obtained an update on his personal care of the horses. At night he walked the decks, always watching the people coming and going front and back of him.

"Horace, I think I will go below and check on my mule and the pups. I will have a long ride up north when we dock on the Texas coast," Jonathan Masters said. His left eye was bandaged shut for a few days letting the incisions heal. On the slow-moving craft, Dr. Lacy had operated to loosen up the tight skin from the scalping Masters had suffered nineteen years earlier. It had been a total success, but it would be a couple of weeks before the stitches could be removed. Moving down the stairs, Jonathan saw a moving shadow in the stall. When he stepped down among the animal's holding pens, he saw the tall Black man brushing a horse. Behind the two men, the crewman Wineseal was cleaning out the mule's stall. "Good evening, Professor Masters," Wineseal said.

Jonathan acknowledged Wineseal and turned to the man with the horses. "Those are fine animals," Jonathan said even before he could see the well-dressed man.

Jo Kline turned to face a redheaded man and realized he was facing a man who had been partially scalped. *'Could this be the red-headed man who drowned the young Apache Dog Head? Surely, this was the man,'* he thought.

Instantly Jo Kline's mind went back to that day. He and his warriors had watched while the red-headed man led the mules away from the wagons just before they had attacked. Shaken to the core, Jo Kline did his best to keep his voice smooth and with as many Spanish-sounding words as possible.

"These are my horses. I buy many and sell to the army. I like the looks of that

112

mule. If he is yours, I would like to buy him! I sell horses and mules to the Mexican army," Jo stated.

Jonathan smiled. The lantern light was not in a good position, and his bandaged eye kept him from getting a good look at the man. He could tell this man had a Spanish background. He was well dressed and had a gold chain that sparkled in the lanternlight. Something about this man made Jonathan apprehensive. He wanted to engage him in conversation, but the big man lay the brush down, rubbed the heads of the dogs, and made his way up the steps to the first deck.

Jo Kline found himself in deep thought as he looked out over the dark water before entering his room. This red-headed man had been walking with the beautiful woman just before a brave had killed her. He had wanted to take the two young women alive, but instead, one had been killed. The brave who killed her was taking her scalp to hang on his lance. Jo remembered pushing him aside when he realized he had been shot by the only man on the wagon train who had a rifle ready. That shot killed the young warrior and stopped an inch into his back. Jo pushed him aside and took her scalp off the dead warrior's lance and all the items Elizabeth Masters carried in her pockets. One was a velvet pouch—his hand went to the gold watch in his vest pocket. The inscription on the watch bore initials. Popping open the cover, he immediately knew that the watch was meant for the red-headed man. The initials were J.M. Surely this was a bad omen. The man's name was Jonathan Masters. How could the two men he had taken so much from years ago be simultaneously here on this same boat? Looking out over the Gulf of Mexico, he realized he was in a situation where there was no place to run for the first time in his life.

Days later, the sternwheeler moved in against the Corpus dock. Bald Jo had been waiting for this very moment. Earlier, he had saddled the big grey stud with the stocking feet. One more hour, and the unloading would begin. He took up his rifle case, studded cane, and carpetbag and reached for the door. Then Jo thought of the book lying on the bed.

Meanwhile, over a chess game, Jonathan Masters watched his opponent Horace Lacy thinking of his next move. "Horace, if you do not decide to make a move, the boat will finish docking. I will declare myself the winner because of your inability to decide," Jonathan said.

"Well, Jonathan, your eye sure looks better," Horace said.

"Horace, you are avoiding the issue. Make your move or I win," Jonathan said.

"In a chess game, you cannot declare yourself the winner. You are just trying to distract me," Horace said. "This game will be continued until I am triumphant, whether it be on land or sea."

It had been many days, and the stitches and bandages had been removed from the side of Jonathan's face. His sight was not hampered any longer. Now that his top eyelid was set in place, his stares were no longer unsettling. "Is that the gangplank going down? Time is running out on this game," Jonathan said.

"While you are trying to finish your game, I think I will go for a walk on the deck," Samantha Lacy said.

"Good!" Horace Lacy said. "Take this annoying Theology Professor with you. He is trying to sabotage this game I am sure to win!"

The deck was wet from the rough water splashing on the main deck, so the two climbed the stairs to the second deck to do their walking. Pulling her shawl tighter, Samantha said, "Jonathan, I am so glad we have had these talks. It has benefitted both of us. I think you and I can both let go of the past and live for the future."

Bald Jo Kline pulled the door open, holding his rifle case, cane, and book. Getting his big frame and carpetbag through the door was difficult. Just at that moment, Samantha Lacy stood in his way. As he got through the door, they came face to face in a moment of stark terror. She started to scream but fainted instead. The shock caused Kline to drop the book as he turned and moved to the lower deck as fast as possible. Caught off guard, Jonathan Masters grabbed her as she fell. The book landed at her feet.

"Samantha, Samantha, what happened?" Jonathan asked.

It took several minutes for her to get her wits about her, with Jonathan fanning her with his hat. Valuable time for Bald Jo. Tying the carpetbag behind the saddle, he slid the sword from the walking cane and, with two swift moves, cut the ropes that held the loading/unloading platform in place. Its falling was loud, but he was riding along the dock leading his other horses in the next instant.

Samantha came to her wits, and laying at her feet was her diary with her name embroidered on the cover. "Jonathan, that was the Indian called Black Hawk that massacred the wagon train years ago and took me," she said.

"Are you sure he is the man? He no longer lives as an Indian," Jonathan said with an icy voice.

"I will never forget that evil face. It was him, alright! He has become a chameleon changing his way of life. Now he is more dangerous than ever. He is still alive and was responsible for Elizabeth's death. He has had my diary all these years," she said, picking up her diary with shaky

116

hands. The excitement had caused a crowd to gather, and suddenly Horace Lacy was standing over his still faint wife.

Jo Kline made his way to the livery on the north end of Corpus. He bought a sack of grain and fitted a mare for a pack there. Next, he went to the store and finished getting all the things he needed for living on the land.

"Will that be all, sir?" the clerk said.

Jo Kline thought for a minute and then said, "There is one more thing."

"Mr. Wineseal, saddle my mule. I must get my things, and I will be leaving as soon as possible," Jonathan Masters said. A few minutes later, Jonathan had gone through the room where Bald Jo Kline had slept. Picking up items that Jo must have handled, he stuffed them in a pillowcase.

Down in the stable area, he prompted Wineseal for other items Jo Kline had handled. Placing all the items in a waterproof bag, Jonathan looked at the puppies and said, "Well, girls, it's time you start earning your keep!"

Next, Jonathan went to the livery and purchased a pack mule. He outfitted himself at the local dry goods store for the long ride ahead. Looking around the store, he nodded his head that he had everything he needed. "Did a big Black man come in and outfit, such as I have done?" Jonathan asked.

That got the store clerk's attention, and he looked up from tallying the cost. "Yes, he did. Would you, by chance, be Masters?" the clerk asked.

"I am," Jonathan Masters said.

"He left this for you," the store clerk said, handing Jonathan the black velvet bag tied with a leather strap.

The time that it took Jonathan Masters to get his gear ready had worked in Jo Kline's favor. He had planned his exit out for the last two days and was on the trail headed north. He had planned to move north until he could head west into Mexico.

Bald Jo Kline thought of the dogs and the red-headed man. This man was much more dangerous than any he had come against. The red-headed man's wife had been killed by his band. This man would follow him to the ends of the earth. Jo frowned to himself. He should have never taken the boat. Now he had complicated his life. He would always be looking over his shoulder.

Mexico was not so far away. He knew the way, for he had been there many times in years past. It would be good to live there and live as a Mexican rancher.

Jo Kline was thinking of a place in Mexico far away in the mountains. The Don had taken him and Isaac Bell there when they were boys. It was a lonely place. Jo and Isaac had been happy there. They had fished and swam the lake. It was a happy time. Kline always wanted to go back there. So, there he would go and live. Maybe the man would never find him there. Jo knew this man would surely come. He would never give up. For now, the rain was coming down, and that would wash away his scent.

Jonathan Masters walked to a small rock fence located beside the store. The ledge was built around a spring. The spring was the reason the town originated at this site. Oblivious to the people who made their way along the street, he untied the leather strap from the black velvet bag and beheld the content. Back 20 years before, he had guessed right about his birthday present. "It was a gold watch and chain," he smiled.

Nineteen years ago, a happy young woman had purchased this present for her husband and had it engraved. Life held hope and dreams of a wonderful life. Now all these years later, Jonathan Masters held the remnant of her hopes and dreams. Touching the button, the engraved cover flew open, revealing the last words he would ever hear from his beloved wife on this side of the grave.

'To my beloved Professor. My Second Fiddle Man.' Tears flooded his eyes. *'Her Second Fiddle man."* Of all the words she could have left behind, these were a statement dear to his heart, and they gave

him peace. Jonathan's mind went back to a day long, long ago.

Elizabeth Ord sat among a group of college students tuning their instruments. Her brow wrinkled as she held her violin strings next to her cheek. The sounds around her were a collection of highs and lows from instruments being tuned before the evening session. It was December, and the orchestra only had two weeks to prepare for the Christmas concert.

"You need help tuning that fiddle of yours?" a voice said.

Elizabeth flinched. Slowly turning, she exclaimed, "Pardon me, did you just call this Stradivarius violin a fiddle? How did an uncouth, culturally back— Oh! Oh! Professor Masters!"

Jonathan Masters stood with a ragged-looking instrument case in his hand.

"Professor Masters, I assume you are just kidding. I take back the uncouth remark. So, you are the new violinist the conductor told me to assist?" Elizabeth asked.

"Indeed I am. It's been a few years since I have played, and I thought I would broaden my horizons and revive my past fiddle playing skills," Jonathan said.

Clearing her throat, she said, rather huffily, "Professor, there are no fiddle players in this orchestra. We play violins here!"

Opening his case, he roared, grinning broadly, "Good, that means I hold First Fiddle Player Chair!" Elizabeth Ord grew pale and stared at the fiddle that the professor drew from the box. At least she was not disappointed. The instrument in the old case was a scratched-up old fiddle. Around her, the orchestra loft had grown deathly quiet. She saw that everyone watched the bushy red-headed professor as he lifted the old fiddle from the case. Eyebrows were raised, and glances were cast around the room.

"Professor Masters, are you going to play that old fiddle in this orchestra. Don't you have a violin to play?" Elizabeth asked.

"I will play it and make a joyful noise to the Lord! My Lord fully expects to hear musical praises coming from this orchestra at this time of year. I am here to use my God-given talent to praise Him. Are you not a child of God? We are all here to praise Him and bless Him, are we not?"

"Too many questions, Professor! We always try to make more than a joyful noise when playing our instruments. We use our talents, as you put it, wherever they come from, and it does not matter what time of year it is," she said smugly.

"Are you not in my Bible class? I must not be teaching God's Holy Word properly if you do not know from whence your talent comes," Jonathan said.

Looking around at the other musicians listening to the conversation, she was somewhat embarrassed. "Well, I don't know how to answer that, so may I just complete tuning my violin before the conductor arrives?" she asked.

"Of course, I need to tweak my fiddle too," he said.

Everyone was so busy watching the professor tweak the strings on his fiddle they did not notice when the conductor entered the room.

"Dr. Masters, I see you have caused your usual stir among the string section. Everyone, if you have not met Professor Masters, make yourself known to him. He was the lead violinist three years ago. Now let us get down to business. Elizabeth, I am sure you don't mind being second chair under the good professor. Now let us get started, shall we?" the conductor instructed.

Jonathan pulled the bow across the strings, which caused Elizabeth to cringe. Then in a total transformation, the conductor tapped his wand. Everyone was deeply engrossed in the music sheets before them. Suddenly the music synchronized into a smooth sound that made the conductor smile. Jonathan was a natural with talent far beyond Elizabeth's wildest dreams. He did not have to use sheet music. The piece just rolled around in his head, and with his eyes closed never missed a note. The fiddle became a great musical instrument in Masters' hands.

The concert pieces fell in place one after the other, and at the end of the session, the conductor sighed with joy. "I believe this will be the best concert ever performed at this college!" he said.

Bowing deeply, the conductor said, "Dr. Jonathan Masters! Professor! Thank you for honoring us once again with your presence. And thank you for showing what a common instrument can do in the hands of a master musician!"

'In the end, the little fiddle became a powerful tool in the hands of a man aptly named Masters. For in the masters' hands, little became much.'

As Elizabeth Ord snapped the cover closed on her violin case, Jonathan asked, "May I walk you back to your boarding house?"

Elizabeth shook her head a profound yes, and the two made their way across campus along Music Street. The street was aptly named for the great music arts building on the corner.

"Well, Professor, you really made me look like a chump. Do you play the piano?" Elizabeth asked.

"I never desired to play the piano," Jonathan said.

"Good, I play the piano and think I will switch to it now that I realize many musicians knew you and what was about to transpire. My hat is off to you. You have talent that far exceeds any talent I may possess, and you all had a good laugh at my expense," she said to anyone who could hear her voice.

"Elizabeth, isn't it wonderful being blessed with such talents? Literally, millions throughout the ages have been blessed, but only a small few have been given such musical abilities. An artist can take a canvas and turn a flat piece of paper into a scene that holds the viewer spellbound in awe. Some are so well done that a winter scene makes the viewer cold or a desert scene makes one thirsty. A musician can play a piece, and it comes from his very soul. A singer can bless people with the gift of singing. That goes for every gift one can think of. Wouldn't you think that the creator of such gifts should be someone you want to know? Before you answer, remember all such gifts are always a positive accomplishment and should be used to bless the creator," Jonathan said.

"Professor, this is a little deep to comprehend after a day such as I've had," she said.

The two had arrived at the boarding house, and Jonathan said, "One more question, and I will let you go inside."

"Alright, so what is your question?" she asked.

Jonathan could see that she was getting disturbed, and he did not want the evening to end with the beautiful girl annoyed with him. "I see this line of talking tends to upset you, so I will end this conversation and bid you a pleasant evening. It's been a real pleasure to meet you, Elizabeth Ord. I hope to see more of you," he said, tipping a make-believe hat and turning to walk away.

"Not so fast, Professor! What is the question you intended to ask me?" she asked.

Turning back to face her, his gaze seemed to be unsettling. "Alright, I have noted from the discussion we have had today you do not hold the idea of a creator with much esteem. So why are you in my Bible class?" he asked.

"Professor, there is a swing under that tree. Let us sit for a few minutes. My feet hurt," she said. Once they sat down, she began to speak, "Professor, I transferred from Union University last year. My mother did not want me to finish my college years in such a liberal setting. I am a few years older than the girls here in school. It took me a couple of years before I decided to go to college. I am your age; that I know because the girls in school here know all about you. You are the youngest professor at Brown University, unmarried, and you are good to look at. There is one other reason—my mother insisted I take one Bible course a year. I cheated! This is my first Bible class. Mother is not happy.

So, I waited until your fall class had an opening. Professor Clark is too old, and his voice would put me to sleep," she said.

"Interesting!" Jonathan said. "I suppose those reasons are as good as I could have hoped for. I was delighted when I saw your name on my class listing. I have admired you from afar. You know you are not hard to look at either! You are downright beautiful. It disturbs me that you have not come to an intimate knowledge of the Lord. You bring a Bible to class, and it has been marked as if someone has been studying it!" he said.

"It is my grandmother's Bible. Just to let you know, I am as good a person as anyone on this campus. I do not see the need to have my sins forgiven. I guess if I'm classed as a sinner, I would be a tiny one. My sins would make a very short list," Elizabeth said.

"I think you really are a good person, and that worries me. You can't see the need. Over the next few months, I have two class goals. The first is to make you see the need to know the Creator that inspired the Bible and His saving plan for mankind. The second is to get you to fall madly in love with me. So, if you don't mind, start calling me by my first name," Jonathan said.

"Okay—Jonathan, but you do realize should I ever meet this God of the Bible you and mother tell me about, He might well make you my Second-Fiddle Man," Elizabeth said with a grin.

Jonathan's thoughts came back to the present. Leaning back against a small tree giving him shade, he remembered the Christmas concert and their only shared Christmas. A few weeks later, they were married. They had left for the west in the early spring on the ill-fated Snow wagon train. Jonathan Masters had never known a happier time than he had experienced being married to Elizabeth. Now he could put his troubled heart to rest. Now she was playing for the King of Kings and Lord of Lords. One day he would be with her again on the streets of gold.

C12 - High Places

It was midday when Bald Jo Kline rode through the lonely hills of Eastern Mexico. He had followed a railroad track that twice took him through tunnels cut through mountainsides—miles and miles of ravaged uninhabited country. Ahead he saw the steeple of a church. Puzzled, he rode by a rail coach parked on a siding. Every indication was that it was occupied. *'This is strange,'* he thought. *'A rail coach this nice here in this desolate place.'* He walked up a long grade that brought him to a point overlooking a pueblo deep in the hills of Mexico. Giving the horses a breather, Jo Kline surveyed the town. At best, this mountain town was the last bastion of civilization in this forlorn country. Nothing human could be living in this dejected place. At the base of a mountain, a pueblo with twenty well-built adobe dwellings occupied the only green spot in the countryside. No doubt the town was settled there for the water that ran from the rocky soil at the mountainside's base. The village center was made of a green patch of grass surrounded by a sea of brown. Close to the mountain, a brick tank held water. The extra water overflowed the tank and disappeared into the sand and rocky soil.

In the center of town, a cantina and church stood. As he rode into town not a soul was out on the town square. *It must be siesta time. There is no one to be seen in the dusty courtyard,'* Jo Kline thought.

To the side of the church, a burned-out adobe dwelling stood. Along the street, the brick walls had evidence of recent gunshots.

He was riding a tall grey stud and leading his string of three mares. The horses quickly dipped their muzzles in the cool water and drank their fill, eyeing the green grass and weeds. The place made him feel uneasy, so Kline removed the thongs on the hammers of his pistols. At this time of day, the cantina cast a long shade to tie the horses in. Looking around, he made his way to the cantina. Jo had to stoop low to enter the darkened room. The bar was a brick affair, constructed well and ran almost the length of the back wall. One side wall was decorated with artifacts from bygone eras: Apache weaponry, Spanish helmets, armor, spears, and swords. The room's ceiling was high and spacious.

Jo realized what he had mistaken for siesta time was, in fact, a situation he had just ridden into. Moving to the end of the bar, he put his back to the side wall and stood facing a window where he could see his horses dozing in the shade. Three men sat at a round table, all facing the swinging doors. They were the welcoming committee, no doubt.

"Buenos Dias, Señor," the bartender said in Spanish. Nervously he held up a bottle of yellow liquor. Jo looked at the dull liquid in the bottles and shook his head no. A Mexican walked in from the street and nervously eyed Jo before saying to the three at the table. "Amigos, they come!" Outside, the sound of galloping horses came as a group of men entered the village. Five men suddenly rode into town, shooting their pistols in the air and waving whisky bottles. Jo Kline heard the word *Comancheros* from the men at the table. Suddenly the five stopped and sat on their horses, staring at the four horses of Jo Kline's standing in the shade. Their horses, lean and gaunt, could not compare to these prize horses. Bald Jo knew instantly what they were thinking.

Taking a drink and wiping his mouth with the back of his hand, the leader of the five dismounted and pitched the bottle to another. Smiling at his friends, he slid his sombrero back and walked unsteadily over to the beautiful grey with the Spanish saddle. Speaking quietly to the other four, he indicated for them to watch the cantina door. "Today, my friends, we will be riding in style," he laughed. Running his hands along the thick neck of the stud, he audibly admired the fine horse and saddle. Reaching over, he untied the reins and put his left foot in the stirrup. With his short legs, he could not get the rest of the way onto the saddle without much struggling. The men in the cantina looked around to see what the big man would do, only to find he was not in the cantina. Bald Jo Kline had slipped out the rear while they were busy watching the small fat Mexican's comical mounting outside.

A loud whistle and the grey began to buck around the circle of buildings. It didn't take long until the Mexican lay sprawled in a cloud of dust. The grey trotted back to the water tank and joined his friends in the shade. Laughter erupted inside the cantina and on the street as well. The little man jumped up and wiped the dust and sweat from his eyes. Mad and embarrassed, he looked around.

Bald Jo Kline had seen hundreds of men like these. Comancheros, evil men with whom he had ridden. Men just like him at one time in his life.

At seeing the well-dressed man standing at the corner of the cantina, the little Mexican's right-hand gun came up, and he fired. It was unexpected, and Bald Jo Kline flinched, and with one swift turn, he let go of a Conquistador's spear he had taken from the wall in the cantina. He had thrown many spears in his lifetime. His mighty arm threw it true, fast, and straight.

The little fat bandito looked down at the heavy spear that had passed through his body as he fell dead in the dusty street. Instantly Jo was firing at the remaining men. The three men in the cantina busted through the swinging doors firing at the four. Instantly, the four split up and headed in different directions. The crossfire stopped all four mounted Comancheros before they could get away.

Bald Jo looked around and saw the blacksmith lower his rifle. He had been the one who put most of the Comancheros down. Nodding to Bald Jo, he turned and walked to his blacksmith shop.

Now men and women came from everywhere. The men quickly took the dead men's guns and rummaged through their pockets. The bodies were quickly removed from the town and taken directly to a lonely-looking cemetery to be buried.

A Mexican came over and smiled. Talking in English, he said, "Señor, I have sent a boy for the doctor. The wound does not look too bad. I fear many more Comancheros will come because we have killed their friends."

Jo Kline looked around at the people. The inhabitants of the town were hollow-eyed and seemingly of little intelligence. Except for the four men that had helped in the gun battle, this town was mainly helpless to whatever came their way. Nothing here could possibly give their lives much reason to smile each day. Bald Jo bent low and entered the cantina holding his bleeding arm.

The town had never seen such a man. Bald Jo dropped a coin on the bar and asked the bartender to give drinks to everyone. One of the Mexicans seated at the table stood and addressed Jo. "Señor, I will speak for you," he said. Quickly he translated what Jo Kline had said. Another man asked in Spanish what Jo's name was as the others moved to the bar for the free drinks. Kline did not let them know he could speak Spanish. In reply, Jo asked a question, "What is the name of this town?"

"Paso Verde," replied the one who knew English.

"You can call me Señor Don Verde," Jo stated.

All laughed when they understood and toasted the benevolent Black Señor Don Verde.

This remote mountainous land was the perfect place to hide from the life Jo had lived as the most ruthless Indian ever to ride the plains.

A woman came into the cantina carrying a doctor's bag and was directed to the big man sitting at a corner table. The instant her eyes located him her face grew pale, and she wavered for a minute. Gradually she got her composure and made her way over to the table. In English, she said, "Take off your jacket and shirt, Señor, so that I can see the wound."

133

No one had noticed her surprised look but Jo. He did not know how to take the shocked look she had given him. Was it a look of recognition or did he look out of place here in this desert town? Standing, he did as she asked him to and sat back down. In the cantina, excited men drank and discussed the great victory against the Comancheros. The woman cleaned the wound and applied stitches to a body covered with scars from previous battles. She made no mention of the obvious and, after finishing, said, "You can put your shirt back on now."

"Señorita, is there a place I can stay and a place for my horses here?" Jo asked.

Without addressing him directly, she called to the man who could speak English, "Mateo, get this man's horses cared for, and he will need a place to stay," she said.

"As you wish, Señorita. I will get his horses to the blacksmith and secure lodging in the room above this cantina," the weathered Mexican said. Quickly she turned and left the cantina.

The next few days proved the Comancheros had friends close by. They came looking for them. Jo Kline had expected their visit and had the village boys stationed out of town on the only two trails they could come in on. Meanwhile, he used the three men, Pablo, Mateo, and Araña, to get the townspeople ready to protect themselves. Late one night, a boy ran into town to tell the Black don that a large campfire was a mile down the trail to the west. Bald Jo gathered the oldest boys from the town and sat them down.

"Which of you are the fastest runners?" he asked," Two of the boys raised their hands. "Very well then. You two leave now and spy out the camp. They will not expect you, so make the count and come back here quickly. I need to know how many men are coming. They are Comancheros. They will cut your throats if they catch you. You must be very quiet. Go now and bring me back the number." Passing his finger across his neck, he said again, "Do not let them see you!" Instantly, the two grabbed water skins and left out at a fast trot.

Looking up at the early darkness, Kline looked back at the four remaining boys. "You four boys will leave as soon as those two get back and we find out what we are facing. I want you to go to the edge of the camp and listen to the conversations. One of you will bring me back all that they talk about. The other three will wait until it is very late, and if there are no guards, slip into their camp and collect a few of their rifles. Get only the ones that are easy to steal away." Jo took a feather from a hat that one of the men was wearing and handed it to a boy. "Lay this where they will find it, so they will think Indians have sneaked into their camp and stolen a few of their weapons. Don't take chances. Beware, they will surely kill you if you are caught. Stay away from their horses. They will be guarded," Jo said.

As an Indian, Bald Jo had used the young Indian braves many times like this and thought nothing of it. They were young, brave, and fast. The first two came back into camp within the hour. There were thirteen men around the campfire. There were thirteen old horses and plenty of weapons. The next boy came in alone, breathing hard from his run, and related all the four had heard from the men.

"They would attack at first light while the peasants were sleeping. Three would carry torches and set fire to the thatch roofs of the buildings. The rest would circle, killing anyone that ran from the burning buildings," the boy said.

Not long before daylight, the last of the boys came back into town smiling. Each was carrying four rifles apiece. They had also collected three bandoleers of shells. Jo smiled and stationed the best shots behind the brick walls of the houses—the best place to fire. Everybody was ready for the attack. The Comancheros did not know a battle-wise man had taken up residence in Paso Verde.

Jo made his way to the blacksmith's shop to check on his horses. The blacksmith stood watching Jo Kline walk across the town proper, headed for his shop. Jo started to speak as he walked up but suddenly stopped. A look of sudden recognition came over his face. The blacksmith spoke in Spanish and said, "It is true, Señor. It is I, Francis Littlefield. I was not sure about you until you threw the spear. You and I have come from the same point in life. We just came from different directions. I don't know why you are here, but it would be best if these simple folks did not know you are Bald Jo Kline the Black Hawk, or I am Francis Littlefield the Comanchero blacksmith. They shouldn't know that I rode with the Comancheros and stabled their horses. I came here looking for a place to hide from my sins," the middle-aged man said.

"Then Francis, our secret is hidden and must not come to light. I do not plan to go back to the way of the Indians," Jo said.

"Neither do I," the blacksmith said before turning back into his shop. "If the Comancheros see us, they will know us," the blacksmith said.

The hoofbeats could be heard as the cock crowed, and thirteen men rode onto the Pueblo green, splitting into two groups they circled the haciendas firing into the black windows. Most of the pistol fire was returned with rifle fire that had a withering effect on the outlaws. So intense was the firing that the surviving Comancheros turned tail and raced as fast as they could out of town. They neither turned back to look or to help their fallen friends.

C13 - Visions in Clay

Months later, a rusty old steam engine labored to get through the hills of eastern Mexico. Bald Jo Kline folded a newspaper and lay it on the table before him while sitting in the dining car. It had been over a year since he had made his exit from the sternwheeler docked at the Corpus Christi Wharf. Finally, he had begun to relax. His new life was falling into place. Bald Jo Kline had made the transition from one world to the other.

The train swayed from side to side through the boulders and cactus-covered countryside. February was usually a mild winter month in this part of Mexico, but it had turned cold with a bitter north wind blowing. The engine only pulled five cars this day. First, was the dining car Jo Kline sat in. Then two stock cars rocked along full of cattle. A string of eight spirited three-year-old mares to improve the already quality stock that Bald Jo Kline had acquired over the last year, was in the next car. His breeding stock had always been selected for size and endurance. The last car had been filled with cut wood, boards, and sticks of all sizes.

Bald Jo Kline had decided not to cross the line again, no matter the temptation. He had become an honest rancher and was at peace with his life as it now was. There was no way to justify the past that haunted him.

As the train rocked along, Kline's thoughts went back over his life to the day he had ridden far out on the plains of Texas to escape the tall man with the dogs. It was a windy, cold day, and he purposed to leave a trail a blind Apache could follow, leading the man with the dogs away from Jo's intended route. Riding hard, he hopefully lured him far out on the Texas prairie before turning back for Mexico. When he turned back, he was wise and made his trail disappear as if he had taken wings on the windy plains.

That was over a year ago. Jo shook his head with a frown; he was only kidding himself. There was little chance this man would ever give up until he had found Black Hawk, the man responsible for the death of his wife. This remote place had been Kline's refuge. Good had happened here, and he decided he would never leave. His heart was changing, and he was beginning to relax and enjoy life.

He felt at home in these lonely hills where only the lizards would want to live. This dry country held two supreme prizes—there was water and clay. There were two springs, one of which supplied the town with water. It came up out of the rocky ground before disappearing into the sandy soil or evaporating in the hot

Mexican weather. The Mexicans had built their town around this life-giving spring.

This day he sat in the dining car thinking. He always occupied the last seat against the back wall. Caution had always been his nature. He never let his guard down.

Kline had once thought there was nothing of value here, but he had been wrong. The people were the one thing he had found of value. They were using the only truly raw material that existed in this barren land, 'clay.' The clay had a unique quality and was dug from a pit. From the town's beginning, the peasants had made pottery, bricks, and ceramic pieces of all sizes and shapes.

Over the years, they had crafted beautiful items by hardening the bricks with fire, making stunning ceramics and pottery. Their skills had been passed on for generations and gone unnoticed by the outside world. Their skills had made life easier in this harsh environment. Using dyes found in berries and plants, they had created beautiful pieces that Jo had only seen the equal to in the hacienda where he had lived as a youth. A feat of engineering he found unusual was a brick furnace where they fired the clay ceramic pieces. Everything that would burn was used for baking the ceramic and clay items. His opinion of the peasants was changing. They had worth! The more he discussed with them the things they made and their ideas, the more he realized they had creative abilities. His assessment of those simple peasants around him had been wrong.

Again, his attitude and thoughts were changing. The book he was reading to make his speech better influenced him in many ways. The book made him realize there was a worth about humanity that was different from all else. Their worth could not be measured in their abilities to fight, kill, or steal.

He had no idea how well the pottery and ceramic pieces would be received by surrounding communities until he took several boxes of the dishes and wares with him on a cattle buying trip.

"Pablo, you, and the men get the things we brought unloaded. I will check with the local merchants to see if they would like to purchase these items," Bald Jo said as he walked away from the railroad station.

Several women leaving the train saw the items that Pablo and Mateo were carefully unloading and immediately began gushing over them. These simple men did not know that items like these appealed to women who knew quality ceramics from Spain that were hard to get. Only one merchant who talked to Kline ventured down to the station in the day's heat to see what Jo Kline was peddling. Upon seeing the women's response, the store owner was instantly convinced and bought every item with the assurance to Mateo that he would purchase everything of such quality.

On their second trip, Jo asked the storekeeper to give him a list of what he needed. A thick picture book was given to Jo to see if they could create the plates and cups in the pictures. Instantly the orders were filled. Mateo had to find more wood so the items could be packaged. Jo was overwhelmed with the amount of money he was able to bank for the people of Paso Verde.

The peasants became industrious, working from daylight to dark, filling the orders and chatting excitedly about designs and new ideas they could create. The furnace never cooled unless the tender ran out of wood. The town's young boys were up from daylight to dark, walking far and wide looking for sticks—anything that would burn.

Jo smiled. He had created a new industry for several towns gathering the unwanted wood close to the tracks. There was wood for fueling the furnace in all the train's towns. A boxcar to carry the wood was designated. Each time the train arrived in Paso Verde, the wood was unloaded and stacked for use. The orders were so plentiful that a very round Señorita was designated to control what went into the oven and when. Old barns were plentiful.

Mateo bought anything that would burn, and Araña kept the furnace hot. A train car could carry a lot of flammable items. Jo took men with him and traveled the rails for months taking the ceramics and pottery to towns far along the tracks. After a very short time, buildings sprang up, and businesses prospered with only one limiting factor—water. Painted clay pots, plates, and cups were all works of art. There were always men with Mateo to carry the wares to the places that had purchased the items, and he kept receipts for each purchase. The men then bought tools and items the town craftsmen and women needed. Letting his sales personnel take over the business for the town's wares, Mateo focused on the distribution of wealth to all that worked while he ran the banking.

For Jo, it had become a boring and lonely ride back to Paso Verde, the place he called home. Something was missing in his life. He dozed in the back of the car while Pablo, Mateo, and Araña chattered about the trip's success. Pablo was fiercely loyal to Jo and took care of Jo's cattle and horses with a crew of men.

Then there was the one they called Araña. As a boy, Araña had not known his mother or father. His thoughts were his own. For most of his life, he had lived in a small adobe filled with spiders on the outskirts of town. So came his name, the spider boy, (el chico araña). Araña had no education. He could not read or write and was unable to speak. He survived by doing errands and firing the furnace that made the peasants' clay pots. Before Jo Kline, Araña's existence was to fire the furnace and search far and wide for sticks and branches. Now he became important in the operations of the various businesses the town was involved in.

These three men were small in stature, and their age was undeterminable. Darkened from the sun and leathered from the dry wind that blew through the mountains and prairies, they now worked for Señor Jo Verde, the Black Don. Their lives had changed and held meaning. One day Jo called them and handed each one a new repeater rifle and pistol. They now carried the best repeater rifles and wore new Peacemaker pistols in a desperate land where such a prize made men of equal stature. They would practice daily with these new weapons in the weeks to come and increase their deadly skills. In the front of the coach, they talked excitedly among themselves. He smiled, knowing they were loyal to him like the savage Indians who followed him across countless miles of prairie and river deltas. He thought of the wealth the town had accumulated.

Always there was the young girl that followed him around town, watching his every move. To Jo she was quietly strange.

At any time she would start whistling a beautiful tune. Often when he was walking along, he would hear her whistling a soft and sometimes melancholy or mournful tune of her own making. She was the daughter of the doctor that lived in the train car. But when he tried to talk to her, she would run away, almost frightened like a wolf or wild animal. So, he just put her out of his mind and went about his business, for many people followed him around town. He was the Don of Paso Verde.

One day in the cool of the evening, Jo rode his stallion along the tracks. He passed the train car shaded by the mountain at this time of day. The two women sat reading at a table in the shade. He was smitten by the woman doctor, Erlinda. On the other hand, she seemed to go out of her way to get as far from him as possible. Jo tipped his hat and was sure he would not be received well. He was right. Instantly the two got up and went inside. At the time, he had mixed feelings about how to approach the two. They always gave him an uneasy feeling. The eyes of the woman had never held any kind of warmth toward him. He decided he must talk with her. He wanted her to know the growing feelings he had for her.

C14 - The Grief of Sin and the Marvel of Grace

On a cold morning, Tindal Sloan, Jonathan Masters, and four other Rangers from company D rode out of Realitos, Texas. The Rangers had been commissioned in 1874 to fight the Indian, Mexican Bandits, and outlaws. Winter was almost over, and a hint of spring was in the air. It wouldn't be long until the grass would be knee-deep and waving in the constant wind, and wildflowers would cover the land. Riding easy in the early morning darkness, they watched for the first rays of the morning to bring light to their side of the world. Jonathan Masters rode his tall black mule. He reasoned that a mule was far more practical than a horse. He used dogs where the rest of the Rangers preferred the speed of a good horse with no other baggage to slow them down. Jonathan's old dog, Gracey, had died. His four pups were no longer puppies. The early morning chill made them want to run.

The Rangers made their way across the prairie, watching the dogs crisscross the open ground in the darkness like shadows. The Rangers could not deny the effectiveness Jonathan had had in his time with the Rangers, but he was an odd sort, and his appearance after being scalped was alarming. He settled back and waited for the glorious sunrise in the eastern sky, giving the mule his head.

It had been almost two years, and he had not heard of the return of Bald Jo Kline or Black Hawk raiding anywhere. Bringing Bald Jo Kline in would be a noteworthy prize for the Rangers. Jonathan had expected to hear of raids along the Texas coast, but that had not happened. The one chance meeting in Corpus Christi had long ago settled back in the recesses of Jonathan's mind. He knew the time would come, but for now, he had been busy bringing in the horse thieves, rustlers, and desperados of all sorts that scourged the western lands. The bounties for the complex cases had been good, and preaching to the different tribes kept him busy.

He had worked as a Texas Ranger. Jonathan was enjoying the company of the likes of Tin Sloan and Uncle Beauregard Staples. The life of a Ranger left him little time to mourn his loss. Two days earlier, a bank job had been pulled in Houston. The Rangers were quick to act. The six men would try and cut them off before they made their way to Mexico or Oklahoma.

The Rangers split up into two groups. Four headed for the Oklahoma crossings, leaving Jonathan and Tin to cover the usual places bandits and thieves crossed the Rio Grande into Mexico.

In the distance, Jonathan saw the twinkle of a small campfire. He corrected the forward motion of the mule to bring him to the fire, hoping for a fresh cup of coffee. The dogs arrived at the campfire first, and they could see a man who was rubbing their ears.

"Hello, the camp!" Jonathan called out. He was hoping to hear a familiar voice. The mule brayed, and then came the reply.

"Let me guess! Could that be Professor Jonathan Masters sitting on the mule outside my camp?" the sleepy voice of Cal Lacy called out.

"The one and only and riding with me is Tindal Sloan. You have me at a disadvantage. I do not recognize the youthful voice," Masters called back.

"Cal Lacy, the son of Horace Lacy. Ride in. I was about to start breakfast, and the coffee is just about ready!" he said.

The loneliness the prairie brought into the life of those who lived there brought happiness upon seeing a friend.

After a greeting, Cal requested, "Tell me all you know of my mother and father!"

Jonathan smiled; his eyes fixed on Cal. "They are in fine shape. I had a long visit with them in New Orleans. They told me what you were up to," Jonathan said. "I want to hear all about your adventure. Your folks live in New Orleans waiting to hear from you. We had quite an adventure ourselves. Ran smackdab into the Black

Hawk! It seems Bald Jo Kline is still alive and well. Now he is living in the civilized world. I was right next to him and did not know him from the other well-dressed gentlemen in New Orleans," Jonathan Masters said.

"Why would Bald Jo Kline be in New Orleans? What is he doing in the civilized world?" Cal asked.

"It is not hard to figure! He is the number one Indian the military wants to put out of business. After our confrontation, your parents and I sat down and tried to determine why he would be in the same town and on the same riverboat as we were. We came up negative, but it is hard to believe he was there by accident. I concluded he was headed to Mexico. With all the troops in the west, he will be the main target if he starts raiding again. Kline's smart enough to know that. It may be that there is something that he remembers from his childhood. In New Orleans, he was dressed in Spanish clothing and spoke broken English with a Spanish accent. At one time, he must have had a life in Mexico. What do you make of this?" Jonathan asked, handing Cal a fancy mug with a picture on it.

For a few minutes, all was quiet. Then Cal looked at the mug in his hand. Puzzled, Cal asked, "Where did you get these cups? This, no doubt, is Jo Kline."

"I never had a real good look at Kline; just heard his voice on the sternwheeler. I came across these mugs, and a trapper told me this was the face of Bald Jo. Just curious, but how do you know this is Kline?" Jonathan asked.

Cal handed the cup back to Jonathan. "Because this picture could well be me. Even the horse is a grey like I ride. I know this is Black Hawk because some time ago, I was scouting and came back to camp to find him attempting to steal horses. I had the drop on him, and he knew full well I would fill him with lead. That did not seem to bother him. He was going to fight us anyway. So, I let him know I was the son he traded for three jugs of liquor nineteen years ago. He was totally puzzled by the encounter, and after studying the situation, he just looked me over and walked back into the bush," Cal said.

"Why did you let him go knowing what damage he has done in his lifetime?" Jonathan asked.

Cal poured himself a cup of coffee and sat looking at the steaming coffee and considered the question. "It is hard to shoot someone in the back, especially when you realize he has just (maybe for the first time in his life) listened to the voice of reason. The Bible says, *'come let us reason together.'* I believe I was doing the right thing. Reason is a powerful force. Mighty pretty cup, Jonathan. Let's have breakfast and ride to the herd," Cal said.

C15 - The Longworth Episode

In the late evening, Jonathan Masters, Tin Sloan, Cal Lacy, and Abel Blackburn stood watching the herd pass by all strung out. "This is the nicest herd of cattle I have ever seen," Jonathan said.

"Well, you are not alone in thinking that. A fellow by the name of Longworth sent a boy to let me know not to move the herd unless I left fifty head behind. He will take the whole herd if I don't," Abel said.

"Longworth!" Jonathan said with a scowl.

"When did this happen?" Cal asked.

"A boy rode in yesterday evening. He couldn't have been more than sixteen. Biding for time, I told him I would give his boss an answer tomorrow, and that is today. Cal, I was waiting for you to get back and for Hank and Joe Bess to get here before I had to face him cold. I just wanted everyone to know what we are facing," Abel said to Cal.

"What's your decision, boss?" Cal asked.

"Hank and his Indians will not be in until the herd is gathered this evening. I have been going over the situation in my mind. The Indians are poorly equipped to fight well-armed men. Most of them are young, and the only weapons they have are

153

sharpened sticks. I don't intend to sacrifice their lives to save the cows. The drovers are good fighting men, but I only have a few drovers. As it stands, I need a plan to win this battle. I do not think this Longworth will be satisfied by taking fifty head. I do not intend to give him any," Abel said.

Jonathan looked around at the young Indian braves walking by the herd with sharpened sticks. A few had bows and a quiver of arrows. There was a scattering of old rifles carried by some, but it was doubtful they knew how to use them. An occasional seasoned drover was moving back and forth, keeping the cows in line. Their destination was a big grassy place where they could hold the herd for the night.

"Abel, unless I miss my guess, this Longworth has already looked this herd over and knows exactly how many fighting men you have. He sees this herd as a ripe plum he is going to pick. You could give him half the herd, and he would still attack you for the rest," Cal said.

"Well, Cal, I am glad to see these fighting men you brought with you. I hope you will lend us a hand with this problem," Abel said.

Jonathan Masters reached in his coat pocket and pulled out his Texas Ranger Badge. "Abel, we would like to ride out with you when you give Longworth your answer," Masters said. Then he pulled a long barrel shotgun from the pack on his mule.

Tin Sloan pulled a long barrel shotgun from a scabbard on his horse and checked the load. "We can discuss a plan after seeing what he has to say. He is not waiting for your decision. He does not want you to get organized. His welcoming committee is waiting for your answer," Jonathan said.

Looking out across the prairie three men sat on their horses. Tin rubbed his chin and spoke, "Abel, I think we can get you some time so you can get you a plan together."

Abel looked at the closest drover. "Red, get the herd settled down over there for today. There is a stream of water just this side of that rise. Settle the herd and get the men ready for a fight if it comes to us today," he said.

As the four rode out to meet the three men sitting on the prairie, Abel asked, "How many men do you think this Longworth has riding for him?"

"Well, the war has produced a lot of hard cases. He sees your herd as already his. He won't hit you tonight. He is smart enough not to want to fight in the dark. Longworth considers himself the law in this part of Texas. He rides with a wild bunch and tries to cut every herd he sees crossing the prairie," Jonathan said.

"We have gone through too much to let anyone cut this herd," Abel said.

Jonathan looked at the three sitting on their horses through his binoculars. "Tin, the two men are wearing masks. The boy looks like he would rather be somewhere else. What you want to bet the masked men are on one of the wanted posters I have in my pack?" Jonathan asked.

"Well, we need to talk with these two and possibly take them into Parker's settlement, either riding their horses or strapped across them," Tin said.

A few minutes later, a group of heavily armed men sat on their horses facing each other. "Longworth said to tell you that you have no options. You have run out of time. Leave a hundred head of cattle, or we will take the whole herd," a masked man said.

Suddenly, the three were facing two scatter guns at point-blank range. "Say, what is this?" one of the masked men asked.

Tindal Sloan sat looking at the masked men before saying, "Gentlemen, this is a moment of decision for you." In unison, Tin and Jonathan pulled back their coat to reveal the Texas Ranger badges. "If you pull your weapons, you will be shot off your horses. Now I want you to remove your masks so we can see who we are looking at."

"Wait a minute! We are under a flag of truce," one of the masked men said.

"Flags of truce are for armies at war against each other, not thieves and murderers," Jonathan said.

Reluctantly, the two men reached up and pulled their masks off to reveal two identical faces. "Let me guess— you are Foster Peals twins, Jessie and Burl. Unbuckle your gun belts with your left hand and let them fall to the ground. According to the wanted posters in my saddlebags, you two have made a name for yourselves. You, boy! Turn your horse around and go back to Longworth. Tell him two Texas Rangers, Tindal Sloan, and Jonathan Masters just arrested the Peal brothers. He will not cut this herd, and if he shoots a Ranger, every Ranger in Texas will be riding out to find him!" Jonathan stated firmly.

As the boy turned his mount, the twins saw their only chance and drew in unison. It was a foolish act committed by two desperate men facing the gallows if they were taken to Parker's Settlement, Texas, to face the hanging judge. Their bodies were turned over to the four Rangers returning from the Oklahoma border.

Days later, drovers assembled around the campfire, getting ready to move the herd. It was a somber mood as today Cal would be leaving the herd with Sloan and Masters. He walked back into camp with Tin Sloan leading their mounts all saddled and ready to ride. Abel was moody and stood next to the wagon that belonged to Cal.

"Well, Abel, it looks like you are going to get your herd home. We missed our opportunity to catch the Sellers gang before crossing the Rio Grande," Tindal said.

"I hate to see you go, Cal. I wanted to have you around my ranch for a few days relaxing. From here, we will be there inside of three weeks," Abel said.

"You will see me soon. I must come back to collect my wagon, mules, and pay," Cal said with a grin.

Cal walked along the line of men standing by the campfire, shaking each hand, and got a bearhug in return. Jonathan Masters listened to each man as they said their goodbyes.

'When a man spends as much time working with a group of men as Cal had, the men should have known a positive influence from working with him. They all knew that he was the son of Bald Jo Kline. Now they realized the blood that flows through a man's veins only gives life to that man. It is the knowledge of being made in God's image that makes the man. Thanks to Cal's mother and adopted father, he could handle and overcome his bad beginning,' Jonathan surmised.

"I want you all to know that it has been a real learning experience working with you men, and I am all the better for it. This is not the end of the trail for us. Remember Modena? Abel's father planted a seed that we were able to help Modena meet his maker as all men should. I will be back to see you all in a few weeks, so this is not goodbye," Cal said.

The men saddled their horses and once again started moving the herd down into the Texas hill country. They had reached the Sheep's Gate by early evening, and Cal rode away with Jonathan Masters and Tindal Sloan. Turning once, he waved a worn and battered old hat, then disappeared, headed for Mexico.

αααααααα

Far along the Rio Grande, a small town had sprung up alongside the rail. Part of the town was no more than a tent city with a collection of Mexico and Texas occupants. One dusty evening two men rode along the main street built along the rails. They stopped their horses in front of the train station and dismounted. One dressed smartly in a long coat, and the other still wore remnants of his Confederate uniform. The most respectful looking of the two made his way around to the window where the telegrapher sat, sending the last messages he had to dispatch of the day.

"Sorry, sir, but I am officially closed. Write down your message, and I will send it first thing in the morning," the telegrapher said.

The man slid his hat back and, with a toothy smile, grinned widely at the man on the other side of the window. "I don't want to keep anyone from heading home, and my questions can wait until tomorrow." Flipping a heavy coin to the telegrapher, he started to walk away, but the man stopped him.

"Just a minute!" he said, picking up the coin and raising the window back fully open. "If it is this important to you, I will be glad to stay a while and send your message," he said. Shoving a tablet across the countertop, he removed a pencil from above his ear and laid it next to the tablet.

"My name is Captain J.W. Dubose, late of the Confederate Army. I own an interest in this trainline that moves merchandise, people, and cattle across the Rio Grande into Texas. I know little about where the things I purchase and ship are on a day-to-day basis. I have decided I wanted to know more about where the purchased materials come from—especially those being shipped from Mexico. You, my good man, probably know more than anyone of who and what comes out of Mexico. So, my need from you is more of an information gathering kind. Questions like where this train goes when it crosses the river. How many towns does it pass through? Where does it make its turn for the return trip back into Texas? The telegraph line runs along the tracks, and surely you know more of what is going on than anyone else. Information on who is traveling the lines, coming, and going, and such would mean a lot to a man in my business. Think on what I just asked, and we will talk more tomorrow. Even the names of gentlemen and ladies who travel the lines out of Mexico could mean a lot of money to me and—you will find I am a very generous man. My friends just call me JW or Captain, whichever you prefer. Good day to you, sir! Now you go home to your family, and we will talk tomorrow!" Tipping his hat, he left the telegrapher speechless, holding tightly to the twenty-dollar gold piece.

As the two men met back on the train platform, the man most in need of a bath said, "Foster, you gave him a twenty-dollar gold piece, and for what?"

Foster replied, "That was seed money. I guarantee you I will know who comes and goes out of Mexico, and we do not have to cross the river to search for Bald Jo Kline. Should he cross the river, we will take him in Texas. There is no reward for him in Mexico, and we could end up in a Mexican prison, which is much worse than the ones on this side of the river. Patience, my good man. Patience. Do not forget. There is a reward for us on this side of the river. I feel better sleeping on the Mexican side of this town."

"No one knows who I am. I do not have a problem with crossing over. It is time we get a bath, and you to dress a lot more respectably. Three days on the plains getting here has made a mess of our appearances. Let us just let the train bring Black Hawk to us. Where do you suppose them two boys of mine have gotten off to? I distinctly told Jessie to make sure they both stayed close to the border so they could get out of Texas quickly. They should have met us here in Reynosa two days ago!" Foster stated confidently.

The two walked off down the main street, not realizing how quickly they would get what they wanted. The name Don Jo Verde would be in the wires.

C16 - A Cup of Tremble

onths before this early morning, Don Jo Verde rode for the town with a purpose. All night he had been restless and lay thinking of a problem the town had. After a good breakfast in the cantina, where he eyed the curtain and the grinning faces of the peasants, he went outside and walked to the source of the town's water supply. His eyes followed the wet sand back up to its origin along the rocky hillside above the town. The new businesses in town had put a strain on the water supply, and he had a thought. This spring was coming out of the side of a rocky cleft and had always supplied the town with the life-giving water—part of the precious liquid vaporized in the hot sun. Even in the cool months, much of the spring water was lost to evaporation and soaked into the sandy earth. Following the water back to its source, he studied it for a while. He sat looking down at the town for a long time and considered the possibilities.

Señor Verde found the answer he was looking for and summoned Mateo. After a short discussion, the little Mexican's eyes were all aglow. Before long, men of the town were enlisted in a project to line a large hole in the ground with bricks and clay. For years this hole in the granite mountainside had channeled a portion of the water away from its downward course to the town. Now the men of Paso Verde would turn it into a cistern to hold water. It would become a tank to hold a large volume of water before going down the mountain to the town.

Other workers made a brick trough to route the water through, which then was covered with brick. It was only a few days before the water coursed through it. The cistern was large, but it took only a few hours to fill. It was then covered with a baked clay dome and a layer of bricks they had made in the furnace. Now the town's water source ran down a covered trough protected from evaporation giving greater access to everyone.

Their imaginations now kindled, they busied themselves in building more brick troughs. With Mateo's instructions, they ran the brick ditches from the storage cistern down along the streets to make it convenient for the townspeople to get water. Several cisterns were built along the downward trek to hold the water needs of the village. Greater access to the water made life easier for the town. The people could carry water for late evening watering of gardens. This ready-made reserve of water supplied two brick bathhouses and a barbershop with cool, clear water at the far end of town in a very short time. At the end of town, the water was still flowing strong and now revived an old stream that, in time, would hold fish and a place for the kids to swim. This quickly became the meeting place for the women of the town. Don Jo Verde became a man of stature like no other.

The second spring was a mile west of town and supplied water for a small lake. It kept the surrounding valley rich with grass. This valley was the location where Señor Don Verde had set up his ranch. Now he enlisted the men of the town to build a bigger clay pipe. He thought of ways to capture and store the water in the valley so the evaporation could be curtailed. The amount of water would then support an even bigger herd of cattle and horses.

The cantina became a busy place where ideas were shared, and plans were made. Their inventions began to sell in other towns. The little train was always carrying heavy clay vessels and pipes ordered by ranchers and store owners along the tracks down the hilly terrain.

The dull eyes that Bald Jo had seen when he had entered the town had been erased. Now new ideas were discussed daily, and with everyone working on new ideas, the small town was abuzz.

Don Verde had started a team of men from the town to build an adobe hacienda in the valley. With only limited building materials, it would take a year to construct a building with high enough ceilings and large spacious rooms to suit Don Jo Verde. There would even be flowing water through his hacienda. He would need maids and men to care for his estate.

A school for the young adults and children was set up, and the local blacksmith soon was teaching school along with his Sunday duties as a preacher.

Such was the new life of Bald Jo Kline, the Black Hawk of the plains. Yet he was apprehensive. He had a nagging realization that all would come to be known about his past.

Bald Jo was amazed by what he had accomplished so easily in this small town by just using his brain for good. He began to regret a past life of using his superior mind to do evil. The thoughts brought back memories of Isaac Bell and his honorable ways. He wished he could see him now.

There was one place Kline never went, and that was the local church. He was certain he could never be forgiven for the evil he had committed. Jo knew one day the tall man with the dogs would find his way to his place of refuge. For now, he enjoyed living and sleeping soundly each night.

There was little entertainment in this small mountain-desert community, and the cantina was the only place to meet. One-night Bald Jo Kline sat in the cantina watching the beautiful young girl dancing.

Her name was Isabella and as she danced her steps were in perfect unison with the whistling she was doing. He smiled to himself at how pretty and talented she was. What had made him smile was the story he had just read that very day from the Bible. The story of a young beauty dancing before Herod the King and asking for John the Baptist's head on a silver platter. The hair on the back of his neck began to rise. Surely his head would someday be offered on a platter.

Unknown to him, the one book that was teaching him to speak well could also teach him about his Creator and the end results of the choices he had made in his life.

Up until now, he had been kept busy by the constant needs of the community. Now they were becoming self-sufficient. His eyes drifted across the room to the woman doctor who stood out above the others because of her height. She was a few years older than Jo knew himself to be and was an older version of the young beauty dancing. Standing, he invited the Señorita to come to sit at his table. Reluctantly she followed him over to the table that was always reserved for him.

She cautiously came to the table but never sat down. For a moment she rubbed her hands together, and cleared her throat, then she said, "Señor Don Verde I appreciate what you have done for the town of Paso Verde. It is the home of my mother and I come here to help the poor peasants with their medical needs."

The don nodded his head at her and said, "I see you are a compassionate woman and there are many people who need your medical help." Jo felt there was a need for caution with this woman. She was surely alarmed and wanted to be away from his table. "I would appreciate if you would look at the man called Araña who is unable to speak, though he can hear," Jo said.

"I will need to examine his mouth to see if there is anything I can do to help him. In the past he has refused to allow me to do so," Erlinda said.

Jo replied, "Señorita, I see no reason why you should not do that. I will bring him to your railcar." He started to speak again, but she had turned and walked away.

Later that day, Don Verde and his faithful companions brought a reluctant Araña to the railcar.

Once inside, Erlinda said, "Araña, sit and open your mouth wide for me. Pedro, bring that lamp over here and hold it where I can see."

Washing her hands in a water bowl, the doctor spoke softly in Spanish. Then placed a towel around his neck and began to examine Araña's mouth.

A few minutes later, the doctor washed her hands, and Jo pulled a chair out for her to sit. "I can fix Araña's mouth so he can talk," she said.

Jo looked from her to Araña and smiled, saying, "Araña, I think you need a voice because you have a lot to say!"

Araña looked up at his don and friends. They all offered him words of encouragement and resigned himself to do this thing.

Jo looked around to find the railcar was well equipped. Erlinda addressed Jo, "Here is where I do my surgeries and the best time to work is in the cool of the evening. With your help, I can operate now, and his tongue will be loosened in a short time. It will only take a few days to heal. Since birth, Araña's tongue has been grown to the bottom of his mouth. I can fix that." And that she did. It took only a few minutes to cut away and separate the skin.

Over the next few weeks, Araña learned to express himself through a voice he never knew he had.

Bald Jo Kline was going through a transformation he never realized was happening. He had developed a genuine concern for the people of Paso Verde. He did not know quite how to handle this type of feeling. In his past life as an Indian, he would just shrug it off when deep thinking beset him. That was not possible now.

A man in the civilized world was measured by his word and lived by what they believed either for good or bad. His uprightness was easy to see, either true or false. Uprightness, Jo Kline had only seen uprightness in the old Mexican Don from his youth and Isaac Bell. Lately, he had been turning to the Book that was increasing his vocabulary and his uprightness.

The book made him think more often than he had realized. Every time he opened the Book just to read and work out more words, something else intervened; ideas and ideals arose. He had just opened the book one day to the Psalms 103:1 and started reading. It immediately made him think about the violent man he had been as an Indian yet gave him hope.

Bless the Lord O my soul: and all that is within me, bless his holy name.

Bless the Lord, O my soul, and forget not all his benefits:

Who forgiveth all thine iniquities; who healeth all thy diseases;

Who redeemeth thy life from destruction; 'who crowneth thee with loving-kindness and tender mercies;

Who satisfieth thy mouth with good things; so that thy youth is renewed like the Eagle's.

He must talk to the blacksmith about this Book. The more he read, the more he felt he had missed a life rich with a totally different kind of lifestyle and usefulness.

One morning he rode up the valley and found the two women reading at the table in the cool of the morning. "May I join you for a few minutes? You have never told me your name?" Jo asked.

The young girl never stayed close when he came near. She got up, and with a small dog that was always in her company, she walked along the tracks throwing rocks.

"She is frightened of me! Why is that?" Jo asked.

"I am Dr. Erlinda McAllen. My father was an American engineer on the railroad and my mother was a Señorita from Paso Verde. My daughter's name is Isabella McAllen. She is twelve. She is a product of an Indian raid on my family's ranch. My father was away, and I was home from school for the Christmas season. It was my last year of med school. No Indians had ever raided that deep into the hill country of Texas. The Indians we knew worked on the railroad with my father and were welcome in our home. We did not know how fierce and dangerous men could be," she said.

It was apparent Jo was alarmed, and his countenance changed. He knew he needed to hear the rest of what she was going to say. Breathing deeply, he said, "Continue with your story."

"The ranch hands were away on a cattle drive. Besides mother and me, the only other person at the ranch was my grandfather," Erlinda said as she took a moment to gather her composure before starting again.

"We had just finished breakfast, and grandfather and mother were milking our milk cow in the barn. I had retired to study in my room upstairs. This week of uninterrupted studying would get me ready for my final semester's test, and I would be able to finish college in early spring. The dog began to bark wildly, and my grandfather looked through a crack in the barn and saw the Indians approaching. He quickly hid my mother and I heard him talking sharply and listened to his final cry of pain. Quickly I looked out of the window and was horrified at what I saw. My grandfather, who I loved so dearly, was dead, his head in a puddle of blood. A small band of Indians was running around the house. I looked at the leader standing in the middle of the corral and suddenly he looked up and saw me and started walking toward the house. I ran around the room and finally, in desperation, crawled under my bed. The one called Black Hawk pulled me from under my bed."

Erlinda looked straight into the eyes of the man facing her and continued, "I guess I would have been killed and scalped had not the horses in the corral broken down the fence, and the band of Indians took off chasing them. I ran into the barn and found my mother shivering in stark fear behind the feed bin. She never recovered and died helpless three months later." Dr. Erlinda McAllen looked defiantly into the eyes of Señor Don Verde. "I was alone with my old grandfather lying dead in the yard. There was no one to help me in my terror and shame. It took me two days to dig a grave in the family cemetery, get my grandfather's body in the grave, and cover it up. Then each night, I relived the horror as I waited for my father to get home. My intended husband, a college professor, shunned and refused to marry me. I was carrying the child of Black Hawk. Nine months later, my daughter was born."

"Isabella, my daughter, will start medical school next year. I managed this tragic time in my life and turned all my attention to Isabella. I have schooled her, and she is ready. She has never been able to attend the local town school. She is the half-breed daughter of the most dangerous Indian in the south country. I was twenty-two years old when this Indian raid occurred. Everyone had heard of the fierce Indian Bald Jo Kline." she said bitterly.

Jo looked at the young girl walking along the tracks. Grief suddenly shot through his soul. He did not want to hear more. He simply stood, took his hat, and asked, "Is it possible that a man like that could ever be forgiven for what he has done?" Not waiting for an answer, he took up the reins and walked away, leading his horse.

Walking away, his feet dragging heavily on the soft sand, he remembered the day. It came back to him like a wave of nausea. He could finish the story. Although Jo did not physically kill the old Mexican, his pallatons were following his orders. While the rest of the band pillaged the house, he found the girl hiding under a bed. The only reason she had been left alive was the frightened horses in the corral had knocked down the fence, and the war party had taken out after them.

When Jo Kline stopped walking, he was standing next to the lake. He had no idea how to address this situation in his life. He had heard people say they were sorry about things. Just saying your sorry would not help considering what he had done.

Mental agony of this nature never existed in the world of the Indians. Nor to men who did not hold mankind as God's special creation.

He let his mind concentrate on things of the day, and for a while, this relieved his mental agony. The day was waning when he headed back to his hacienda. A boy came from the barn and took the bridle of his horse. Walking along the lake, he watched cattle and horses grazing in the moonlight like shadows. Shaking his head, he gave up the day and retired for the night.

Before sunrise, Bald Jo Kline ventured out of his newly built adobe hacienda and walked along the lake. He heard the crunch of footsteps in the sand behind him. "Señor Don Verde, may I finish our earlier conversation?" she asked.

Jo Kline turned and, without saying a word, nodded for her to continue.

"Each year, I came here with my father, and my heart went out to the poor peasants of Paso Verde, so once a year, I come and do what I can for the people here. On this trip, I was amazed at what I found happening here. I find it is all a work of your great mind. I cannot see how this could happen. I know who you are. Now I find you are not only alive but not what I have hated all these years. I believe God has shown me firsthand what he could have done with you had you not turned savage in your youth. The life of an Indian is directly opposite from the life of a Christian. You have done much for the people of this poor, remote village. I hope your presence here will always be a positive thing."

"I had to explain to Isabella why she had no father at home and who her human father was. She put things together when she saw you and figured out who you were. Now under bitter circumstances, I must try and help her understand how it is possible that a man can do the things you have done as an Indian, yet she sees what you are now to the people of Paso Verde. You have started the nightmares all over again. God has brought me here now, so I can see his handiwork in your life, but I can never, never, never, forgive you," Erlinda said.

ααααααα

Weeks had passed. While traveling on the train for a business trip, Jo Kline was contemplating his conversation with Erlinda. He had not had the courage to face her. She was ever present in his mind, especially since the lights of her rail car could be seen at night from his hacienda. Jo was more vulnerable with his emotions at night when he was not occupied with the ongoing growth of Paso Verde. He rubbed his cold hands together to generate a little warmth as the train rocked on.

With one act of grateful appreciation from the townspeople, everything would soon start falling apart, and disaster would soon befall him. He knew the townspeople held him in the highest esteem, which gave him a warm feeling. He thought of the curtain covering the side wall in the cantina. It had covered the wall for weeks. Thinking back, he had grown accustomed to the curtain that covered the wall. The three amigos were in the front of the car carrying on a quiet conversation.

Mateo was exceptionally cheerful that morning for some reason. Jo started putting it together when they rode into town and found that the entire square was decorated around the cantina.

"Well, boys, it looks like we will have a fiesta. Do any of you know what this is all about?" Jo asked, knowing from their faces they were part of what was up.

There was instant denial all around with broad smiles as the four dismounted and entered the cantina. The cantina was well lit this morning, and the entire town was there wearing their Sunday best. At the end of the bar, the blacksmith stood wearing his finest clothing. He stood behind a makeshift podium, and it was obvious it had been delegated to him to make a speech on this momentous occasion. Don Verde was escorted to his favorite table and asked to sit. The people of Paso Verde backed away until they had formed a large half-circle around him.

"Alright, what is this all about?" Jo asked, smiling broadly.

Mateo called for quiet and signaled the blacksmith to make his speech. A somewhat reluctant blacksmith pulled at his tie, cleared his throat, and waved his hands about as he spoke with great pontification.

"Señor Don Verde, it is a great honor that I have been selected to bestow on you this day. The position as the Most

Honorable Man of Paso Verde. In an agreement among the townspeople, you are a saint sent to Paso Verde to help the people, much like the Christ we all worship. The town believes you to be a man given much wisdom from God."

"In the church of Paso Verde, you have been loved and prayed for every Sunday. Today they are declaring it to be a sin for the church of Paso Verde to meet without praying for the salvation and well-being of Señor Don Verde, a man sent from God. A man who has never taken anything from anyone but given much for the well-being of the citizens of Paso Verde. We ask that you accept this small token of our appreciation and admiration for the loving care you have extended towards these people." A young boy came into the room carrying a large box wrapped with colorful paper. Francis cleared his throat and started again.

"The people of Paso Verde declare you must be given the highest respect by all who live in Paso Verde. The citizens declare this day as Honorable Don Jo Verde Day, a day of celebration each year forever."

The blacksmith smiled at Jo and indicated he needed to open the package. Jo was struck with an emotional feeling he did not know how to handle. Peeling back the wrappings, he found a beautifully leather-bound Bible and a smaller package that held a costly pocket watch. His eyes misted, and he could not read the inscription on the watch.

"Señor Jo Verde, on behalf of the people of Paso Verde who hold you in great esteem, we do declare and establish this day a day of appreciation and recognition of all you have done for Paso Verde. Recognition comes from the heart of all who live here, and with a great amount of effort and love have produced this mural to commemorate this event." Francis nodded his head and several of the men, with great care, began taking down the curtain that had covered the work the town's artist had been doing for the past few months.

The painting on the Cantina wall, when unveiled, was a commemorative picture of Bald Jo Kline sitting astride the grey horse. It was a magnificent picture with the day and year affixed. In fact, it was so well done it could be no doubt who it represented. Unfortunately, it could only show the outside of a man they had grown to love. A man who had brutalized many people for the past nineteen years.

Again, the blacksmith cleared his throat and looked at Jo with one eye cocked. "Also, my modest and valiant friend, there have been hundreds of plates that carry this very picture, sold, and released last week. The little train we travel on has carried the dishes with the portrait of you far and wide declaring this day in the south lands. All will see your picture and know the story of your years here at Paso Verde. Yearly they will come to celebrate this day with the town folks."

Jo Kline's chin dropped. His eyes were locked with the blacksmiths. The blacksmith nodded a yes to the disbelief of Jo. He knew what the blacksmith had just implied. The town had signed his death warrant by trying to honor their Don.

That evening Jo Kline entered the church for the first time to find the only Comanchero that had ever turned Christian preacher waiting for him. Jo sat in the second pew and leaned his arms on the first. "I like your church. It has a peaceful air to it," Jo said.

"Jo, it is not my church. It is the Lord's church. I am glad you are here," Francis Littlefield said.

"I apologize for that. I figured your words would be wasted on one as bad as me." Listening to the commotion and music coming from outside, Jo said, "Our friends are having a grand festival outside, Enjoying Honorable Don Jo Verde Day. Francis, I believe I should have come to see you a month ago. I have been agonizing over what I have read in the Bible. Is it possible that I can be saved?" Bald Jo asked.

"Is this Black Hawk backed in a corner talking? Or is this a truly repentant

Jo Kline talking? Before you answer, think about it for a while. I want your answer tomorrow at church!" Francis Littlefield said.

"What time does the morning service start?" Jo asked.

"The service starts at 9 a.m. It will end before the heat gets too bad for the well-dressed," Francis Littlefield said.

Jo heard a rustle in the back of the church and turned to see Erlinda and her daughter sitting in a dark corner, rise and leave.

That night Jo Kline tossed and turned in his bed. He realized there had to be a special worth to human life. God had breathed a part of Himself into every person made in his image. There was no way Jo could go back and rectify the damage he had done. He realized there must be a God and that God would indeed be bound to avenge those who needed justice. Men were not animals. They could make conversation, reason, and build. No other creation could do such things. Therefore, surely, he would have hell to pay.

Sunday morning brought an early morning fog that was thick and wet. Bald Jo had slept a fretful sleep. How could a book take down someone so fearless? He rode along slowly, thinking of what he would say. He was pulled by a force he did not understand. Suddenly he pulled his horse up and sat looking at the rear of the railroad coach, slowly being pulled away from where it sat. The train had a schedule, and it came and went early on Sundays. This time his heart sank. So, what did he expect? He had caused great grief in Erlinda's life. He would have liked to have had one more conversation with Erlinda.

The coach rocked back and forth as the train moved off the spur and headed for the main track where the rest of the train sat waiting. Slowly it disappeared into the fog until only the sound of the iron wheels sounded in the distance. Jo rode into town to the sound of the church bells ringing. His heart was heavy for Erlinda. He had hoped things would have worked out differently.

C17 - *Birds of a Feather*

Three riders sat on their horses in the slow moving water of the Pecos River. "We are mighty close to being in Mexico. Especially for Texas Rangers," Jonathan said.

"Well, we missed the bank robbers. No doubt it was the work of Joe Sellers. He had James Polk and Hasty Fletcher with him. Those two were identified. The Fletcher boy has started his criminal career early in life. You can bet that the rest were John Allen Murphy, Eddie Baker, and the Smith boy; his first name is Toby, best I remember. Sellers is getting brave and keeps making the same mistakes. He always runs to Mexico or Oklahoma. I think this time he went to Mexico. I just need to find out where he crosses the border and cut him off next time he pulls a job. Let's set up our camp over by that bluff," Tin Sloan said.

"You plan on going into Mexico?" Cal asked.

Tin Sloan replied, "We are this close, I figure we all three will...but not with these badges showing. I am just going in to check with some friends who would know where Sellers comes across. It may be a year, or it may be longer, but mark my word, Sellers and his entire band will be the guest at a necktie party.

Jonathan stripped his mule of saddle and bridle and walked back to the small fire. He said, "It's hard to find firewood around here. We need to find some to make morning coffee." Reaching into his pack, he retrieved a plate he had taken from one of the dead outlaw twins saddle bags. "Cal, take a look at this picture. Is this a painting of you on this plate?" Jonathan asked.

"It could pass for me, but this must be a portrait of my biological father," Cal said.

"This is very interesting. Is it possible a person can change from a savage as bad as Bald Jo into a completely different person? It just does not make sense!" Tin said.

"Black Hawk was reared in Mexico, and now he has left the Indian way of life and returned to Mexico. Strange as it may seem," Cal replied.

Tin Sloan rubbed his chin and considered what he had just heard. "Cal, you had him in your sights and did not shoot. Why?" Jonathan asked.

"The idea of back shooting him did not set well with me. Since that meeting, I have never heard of him on any raid with any band. I want to see for myself if our meeting made a difference," Cal stated.

"Well, I don't think it's possible," Masters said.

The following morning the three crossed the Rio Grande into a large town that bordered Texas and Mexico. It was a wide-open town with no limit to what a man could buy had he the means. "Let us start here and see if we can get a lead on which way to go. I do not understand how you can get your picture on a plate! Cal, you take the stores on this side of the street. I will take the other side. If we see the dishware in any store, the merchant should know from where they came," Jonathan said.

Paso Verde was the first place mentioned by the merchants. Señor Don Verde was well known, loved, and admired in every town they passed. They picked up bits and pieces of his life in Paso Verde as they followed the trail through the eastern mountains. By the time they reached Paso Verde, they were totally amazed at what they had heard. They appeared on the hill over Paso Verde the Sunday morning Bald Jo Kline was being baptized in the center of town. They stood and watched the crowd of peasants sing in Spanish as the largest man in the whole town was baptized. As Jo came up from the water, the citizens around wept openly. The three looked at each other in amazement.

"Do you believe this?" Jonathan Masters asked. Masters released the dogs as the festivities began anew. Bald Jo moved over and sat down on a small ledge by the town's newly erected fountain and dried his face. The dogs immediately ran across and gathered around him.

Jo never looked up at the three men walking through the crowd. He simply gathered the dogs and patted each one talking to them. They had remembered him from the tenderness he had shown years before on the riverboat.

Cal sat down beside him by the fountain and took off his hat.

Jo Kline looked around at the three men and said, "I wish you had come earlier. You missed a good service!"

Jonathan Masters took off his hat and scratched his scarred head, and said, "Is it possible that you have a twin brother?"

"No, I am the very one you seek. I am glad it took you so long to find me because this is the greatest day of my life!" Jo exclaimed.

Behind them, the blacksmith preacher walked up and introduced himself. "My name is Francis Littlefield. I am the blacksmith and preacher here in Paso Verde. Gentlemen, a special table has been set for the Señor. Would you please join us as honored guests for a special meal on this special day?"

"I don't know just how to handle this," Jonathan Masters said.

"Truly, the Lord works in mysterious ways. Through my confession, the people of Paso Verde just today found out that their pastor was an ex-Comanchero and the man who had done so much for this town is none other than the famous Bald Jo Kline, the Black Hawk," Francis said.

That morning the three men watched in amazement as the town honored Jo Kline. While on a distant hill James Polk took his field glasses down from his eyes and turned his mount away from Paso Verde.

While they all sat around a large table, Jonathan was in deep thought, and they sat in total amazement.

"This is not what I expected to find. After all I have lost, I do not know if I can forgive someone who has taken everything from me. Is it possible to forgive a man for the death of someone I loved so dearly and the disfigurement I will have to live with for the rest of my life?" Jonathan asked.

"Professor Masters, are you asking me or asking yourself? I can tell you that I have realized that the way I have lived deserves death. I rode wild and free, not concerned with the lives I altered forever or destroyed. All I ask for is your forgiveness. If you hang me from the nearest tree or let the authorities in Texas do the job, I still only seek your forgiveness. Calvin, that goes for you as well. If it makes you feel justice will be served, then take me back. Just forgive me for what evil

I have done to you and your mother. That is what I ask," Bald Jo Kline said.

Tin Sloan sat across the table deep in thought before speaking. "Kline, you realize that the mural behind me and the pictures circulating across the south on plates will bring every bounty hunter in Texas this way?" he stated.

"I realize that, and I do not know what I can do about it. You came looking for me, so maybe we can settle this, so no one else comes looking for me," Jo said.

"The reward for you Dead-or-Alive is very high," Tin said.

C18 - Reflections

D on Verde sat at his table with Francis Littlefield in the center of the cantina. Francis leaned into the table as he listened closely to the exchange. When there seemed to be a bit of a lull among those sitting there speaking, he said, "I would suggest a funeral and burial. Jo has a new life in Christ, so maybe a funeral and burial would not be out of reason. The people of Paso Verde could help. A fine sculpture by the people of the great Don sitting on the grey horse could cover the place of internment. I have been thinking about this for a while. So, when we buried an old man last week, I made sure he was buried apart from the others in the cemetery so the town could make a monument for Jo if the need arises. The way I see this, we need to approach a neutral party in authority with all the evidence of Jo's changed life and ask for a pardon," Francis Littlefield suggested.

"A pardon for Black Hawk! I figure that would take years, and in the meantime, the bounty hunters would probably make good on killing Jo Kline and collect the bounty," Tindal Sloan said.

"On the other hand, if we take him across the river into Texas, a vigilante mob will surely burst him out of jail and hang him. I must admit I came here to do exactly that," Jonathan Masters said.

Cal sat silently looking at his father. Across the table, Bald Jo sat listening to the conversation and occasionally glancing at his son. "What are you thinking, Cal? We have heard nothing from you," Jo said.

Cal smiled and laid his napkin next to his plate. "I have been thinking only of the absolute difference I have found in you. I believe it would be wrong not to try and get something worked out. For you to spend the rest of your life in a dingy Texas prison would be far worse than me putting flowers on your grave. I think you need to turn your ranch over to your three friends here and disappear until a possible pardon can be obtained. These town folks have learned to survive in this new life you have made for them. Your ranch will be well cared for. If no pardon comes, you can stay out of Texas and fend for yourself in these mountains. You have a powerful witness to share and a beneficial way of helping people that may assist in the survival of the remote Indian tribes of Mexico. What you have done here in Paso Verde is quite remarkable," Cal said.

"Professor Masters, to understand this, it would have to be put down on paper by one who knows and has been personally hurt by the life of Jo Kline yet is willing to forgive and speak out for him. I think that should be you," Tindall Sloan said.

The day was festive, and Señor Don Verde was treated like royalty, and everyone who sat at the table was treated with great respect. The talk subsided until after the meal, and Francis Littlefield declared the festivities were finished.

Jonathan Masters walked away from the rest to find a place where he could come to grips with what he had learned today.

"Pablo, you and Araña make sure our guests are settled at the Hacienda. They will be staying for a few days as our guests. Care for their horses and packs. Get their rooms supplied with warm water so they can bathe. Señor Littlefield, I would like to have your company, too," Bald Jo stated.

"It would be my pleasure," Littlefield said.

"Señor Don Verde, I will get this taken care of right away," Pablo said as he moved quickly away to talk to some of the women.

Looking at Cal and the two others, Jo said, "I would like to know you. There is nothing in my life that I can look back on with pride. I have only known men like me since my youth. Understanding you might help me understand why you would be sitting here and not having already killed me. Since I entered the White man's world, I have been face-to-face with a different type of man. First, there was a blacksmith I happened to meet when I first left the life of the Indian. He made me understand I had to change my way of thinking. The Book with the ten commandments helped me understand how to act in this civilized land. You might help me justify how I feel and the changes that have come over me. I want to know how men that know the White man's God came to be. I can truly say there are very few of you. I realize this hope I have of living a normal life in peace is not possible. My sins are too great to overcome, and I feel sure a bounty hunter will end any hope I have for a future. I believe my life can only end as violently as I have lived. I know this is only right, and I am okay with that," Jo Kline said.

"There were many in the Bible that will show you how God can forgive. You need to know the story of King David and his forgiveness," Jonathan Masters said.

"We will accept your invitation to stay for a few days because we have some very good news for you," Jonathan said.

For the next week, Jo Kline and Francis Littlefield listened to the life stories of Jonathan Masters, Tindal Sloan, and especially how Calvin Lacy had been raised. Kline realized he had been the devil in their lives. Jo said little of himself. After all, what could he say? Nothing could console the men he had caused so much hurt. There were great discussions over the Bible, and the three realized that Bald Jo Kline's brain was a sponge that was soaking up the information. There was story after story of men and women that God had forgiven. This book was written for sinners, as the White men continually call themselves. Jo wanted to know the character of such a God as the Great I Am.

One morning, the breeze blew out of the south for a couple of days, and the rain started. Tindal was glad he had not left a few days earlier as he had intended. A wet camp on the trail is never a comfortable time. As they sat on the patio watching the rain come down, Jo had one request of the men. "Since I have become a new man, is it only fitting that I keep my new name as Señor Don Jo Verde? I want never to be called Jo Kline or Black Hawk again. The old name had too much evil and hate attached to it.

The three men agreed that addressing him as Señor Don Jo Verde was more to their liking. That evening the four men proposed a plan to see if the Texas Legislature could grant a full pardon to Jo. The three would ride for Texas with the hope of finding a sympathetic ear in the public arena. A pardon would give Señor Don Verde the ability to move about freely in Texas and Mexico. In a week, they could cross the Rio Grande.

Professor Masters documented everything he had heard of Jo's conversion and the remarkable help he had been for Paso Verde.

"It might be a good idea for you to turn the operation of your ranch over to Pablo and head into the hills for a few months. Bounty hunters are certain to head for Paso Verde as the plates are circulated," Tin Sloan said.

Jo considered the request and thought for a while. "If I leave the town, the bounty hunters would take out on Paso Verde what should be coming to me. I could not let that happen," Jo said.

A week later, the three prepared to leave for Texas. Don Jo Verde called his trusted friends together, and they walked to the barn where the horses were kept. After a few minutes, Jo said, "My friends are saddling your horses and getting your pack horses ready. Come with me and we will have one last breakfast to get you on your way." After breakfast that morning, they walked outside to find their horses standing next to a fine set of new horses with their saddles on them. "Professor Masters, you prefer a mule, so I have this fine animal for you. He is a gentle but great steed like the one I envisioned King David riding in the Bible stories. Tindal Sloan, your horse looks to have had a hard life. It would be my pleasure if you would take this great mare. She is bred and will bring you a colt that will surely be a quality animal. Cal, this is my greatest stallion. He is young and fast. He has the markings of your grey, and together you will have a pair of quality horses to carry you anywhere you desire to go. Please accept these animals, and I hope they serve you well," the don said.

Two weeks later the three rode across the Rio Grande.

Upon arriving in Austin, Tin Sloan and Jonathan went to the local authorities and collected the reward for the Peal twins, Jessie and Burl. Cal went to the railroad station and wired his parents where he was and encouraged then to join him. Then he began the search for politicians that might help them get a hearing in the Texas Legislature for the most frightening name to be muttered among people along the hills of Texas, Black Hawk!

This was not the first request of this nature before the Texas Legislators. It was, however, by far the most noteworthy.

As days went by, a hearing was set for Jonathan Masters to present the case for a pardon. The idea that Don Jo Verde could be instrumental in helping to make peace with the tribes was a significant factor in the request for a pardon.

The legislature was amazed that an educated man of Dr. Jonathan Masters character and appearance would stand up for a man that had been instrumental in disfiguring the professor so badly and responsible for his wife's death. The fact that the very son of Black Hawk stood between the most decorated Texas Ranger and Dr. Masters held much sway in the decision to grant a pardon.

C19 – The Hills of Home

Abel Blackburn stood in his stirrups and scanned the distant prairie. As far as the horizon there was a sea of grass waving in the wind. It was still miles to the hill country. Two specks were moving across the grass on the horizon. Smiling to himself he was relieved to have Hank Lightfoot and Joe Bess riding point. He missed Cal but these two would more than make up for the loss of him. He could still look forward to seeing him at the ranch in the future. An hour later Hank and Joe came in to view and the two signaled a greeting by waving their hats. While the three stood in the knee-deep grass letting their horse's graze, the jingle of trace chains from the wagon could be heard as they moved across the smooth prairie.

"Abel, let's bed the herd down here. The grass is sparse further ahead. There is a cool spring flowing over there," Joe Bess said.

The herd was allowed to spread out on the prairie and the sound of leather straps and saddles hitting the ground signaled camp was being made. Red made the first round checking the herd just as dark fell. The campfire was small due to the sparse amount of wood the cowboys were able to find. Finally, all was settled down and it was not long until the smell of beans and salt pork was in the air. Suddenly Red rode into the circle of men and dismounted. The look on his face indicated there was something on his mind. "Abel, I know you cannot see it sitting around this campfire, but you better take a look at the sky ahead. There is a mighty big fire up ahead and its spread out," Red said.

The drovers spread out in the darkness and stared into the night sky. "It is a long way off but that is a fire. Something is burning and its right in the direction we are headed," Hank said.

"Abel, I need to ride ahead and find out what is burning. Whatever it is, it started recently because early today Hank and I were not far from that location. We do not want to run into a bad situation tomorrow evening," Joe Bess said.

Abel bit his lip and knocked the dust from his hat, and said, "Alright, you and Hank go. Take a couple of Hank's best warriors with you. I cannot give you extra horses so you will have to spare the ones you will be riding. We will be coming your way tomorrow so, as soon as you can, let us know what we are headed into," Abel said. In just a short time the four men rode out of the camp into the night. With fresh mounts the four rode in darkness letting their horses pick the path they were traveling, always headed for the light in the night sky.

By midnight the four had positioned themselves on the edge of a valley looking into the firelight furnished by burning wagons. The wagons had been caught by surprise. Strung out across open ground they were easy pickings for the overpowering number of Indians. Hank spoke to the braves and the two disappeared into the night. "This is a pretty good place to leave the horses. Hobble them and let's move over where the shooting is coming from," Joe Bess said.

It was a while before the two braves got back to where Joe and Hank were watching the valley floor. One was carrying a new scalp and lance. The other was carrying a repeater rifle and a bag of shells. They had much to tell of what they had found. There were ten wagons. Three were not yet burning because two of the three were carrying a peddler's supply of whisky. The fighting with the remaining settlers had been reduced to just keeping them pinned against the opposite canyon wall. The settlers had taken up a defense behind three burned out wagons and three teams of dead horses. Down the line of wagons, the rest of the war party was enjoying the abundance of firewater the like of which they had never seen before.

Hank pointed to a woman's body that lay a few yards out in the open. "The woman didn't make it to safety before she got an arrow in her back."

Joe Bess and Hank lay prone behind a thick outgrowth of cedars and studied the situation. "Hank, the woman is still alive. Her boot just moved. They are using her as bait to lure someone out to try and help her. I would bet there are several Indians up on that flat area just waiting for someone to be foolish," Bess said.

Hank turned to the Indians who sat behind them admiring the fine rifle. They had taken it from an unsuspecting Indian asleep with a half-drunk bottle of whisky in his hand. While Hank talked, the two looked from the prostrate woman to the bushy high place across from those hiding in the canyon. Then they quickly left in the darkness.

"It's hard to tell how long those hiding behind the dead horses will last but I would bet come daylight some Indians will be above them dropping heavy rocks down on them. They cannot defend the place where they are held up. We need to get word to them. Let them know they have help and we are out here in the dark whittling down the opposition," Joe said.

"Joe, you write a message, and I will shoot an arrow with the note tied around the shaft," Hank said. Pulling his bow, he squinted in the dark looking in the firelight for the best place to stick the arrow. "Now the trick is to stick this into that white horse lying closest to the pilgrims without being killed by a very good marksman," Hank said.

The two Indians came back. This time each with a repeater rifle and carrying everything they could including a set of pearl handle pistols which were the latest Colts. There was plenty of noise down the line of burning wagons as the entire war party was getting drunk. Hank looked at the new weapons that were being admired by his warriors and considered. These weapons used to belong to the pilgrims laying out in the firelight. They came west well prepared to defend themselves but did not get a chance. Talking in the Indian dialect he pointed to the extra rifle and the set of pearl handle guns. Crazy Eye looked at the bounty he held in his hand and considered what Lightfoot had said. Slowly he handed the pistols and one of the repeaters over to Hank and the two locked their right arms. "Hank did you just do a swap for those new pistols?" Joe Bess asked.

"I did Joe! There is not one of us that can make these pistols work for us but you. I just traded the colt of Dancer for those pistols and the extra rifle for you," Hank said.

"You got beat but right now I will feel mighty good wearing those pistols. By the way the arrow with the note had been retrieved," Joe said.

Again, the Indians who were supposed to be watching had gotten drunk so Crazy Eye and Short Feet had just eased up on them and killed them without so much as a yelp. Getting that much weaponry so easy made these two Indians feel as rich men and they would be honored in the teepees for years.

"We need to go up on that hill and make sure there are no more Indians guarding the folks behind the barricade. We cannot send back for help so our help must come from those hiding behind the dead horses," Joe said. Suddenly, a single rock came bouncing across the ground from the people with a message tied to it. The one who had written the note had been overjoyed to see the signature of Joe Bess and Hank Lightfoot on the note attached to the arrow. They would hold steady until Hank and his Indians had cleared the brushy area along the grassy hill.

"Somebody back there knows us," Joe said. The note went on to say they would all move over to the ravine south of their present location. The woman in the middle of the canyon was not dead, and they needed to get medical help to her quickly.

The Tonkawa warriors had proven to be foolish. Their number had been much superior to the wagon train's number, but the liquor had been their ruination.

Joe Bess walked over to the woman and picked her up gently. Once the people saw him pick her up without getting shot the rest of the people quickly moved out of their place behind the dead horses and quietly moved to a ravine. It was not long until the men were having their first face to face with Joe and Hank. Most of the people from the wagons had just abandoned them. They ran to the group making a stand behind the four wagons where they had established a fighting defense. This brought the number to 12 well-armed men. An elderly woman stepped up to Joe and Hank, and said, "This is not the first time you two have come to my aid. My name is Silvia. Is Reddy. with you? I rocked him to sleep when he was a baby," she said.

"Reddy is down in the hills. Now let's see if we can get away from here with our hair." Joe rubbed his chin, and asked, "How many Indians do you suppose are out there?"

A tall man stepped over and introduced himself. "I am William Dove the wagon master and Silvia's husband. We are vastly outnumbered and they are well armed. We have expended most of our ammunition and just about ready to use these fine rifles as clubs."

Hank said, "Joe, the boys riding the herd need horses in the worst way. The best way to handle this is to try and steal the Indian's horses and all of us hightail it for the herd." Hank took his two braves and eased out into the darkness. Just out of the fire light of the wagons they found the horses hobbled. The number of horses indicated there was a larger than expected war party dancing around quickly built fires. At least half of the Indians were laying out on the prairie passed out from the liquor. There was still a well-armed fighting force that was not drunk. Back in the darkness the horses were being led away and it was not long until all were mounted and leading several Indian ponies. Making sure they had gotten out of ear shot, they eased the horses into a lope following Hank and his two Indians into the night. Dawn came and to the surprise of Able and the drovers, Hank brought the horses into the remuda. "Well now Abel, did someone say we needed horses?" Hank asked.

"I remember someone saying God would supply horses and it sure looks like we have a lot to be thankful for," Joe Bess said.

C20 - A Dark Wind Blows

Austin had its share of hard cases, and the streets were filled with men wearing the remnants of the Confederate uniform, ready to fight at the drop of a hat. Most politicians had hired men to escort them back and forth around the city. Open discussions in the city streets often led to gun violence, and the military had to step in and quell the violence. It was a tumultuous time in the streets of Texas.

After granting the pardon, the legislature wanted the now Señor Don Jo Verde to present himself before the ruling body to be presented the pardon in person. It would mean that the Don would have to travel by train across a vast amount of wild territory to get to Austin. A telegram was sent, and Jo and his three friends Pablo, Mateo, and Araña left the following morning, hoping to meet the three in two weeks on the streets of Austin.

Francis Littlefield sent them off with a prayer and hope for the safety of all concerned. He was deeply concerned for Jo's safety.

Francis pleaded with Jo not to go to Texas. It was a long trip and the decision by the Texas legislature had hit the headlines and started a storm of protest around Austin. This political wind made many in the legislature very thoughtful over their decision to give clemency to such a notable Indian.

In a small border town Foster Peal and Blackie Holt made their way down the narrow street to the train station. The telegrapher always had plenty of information, but it was never the name that the two wanted to hear. "Why don't we just go round up those twins of yours and head for the town where this Don Verde lives. The four of us could surely take Black Hawk and cross the mountains back into Texas. I don't like the fact that Tindal Sloan's name popped up as having crossed the river into Texas this morning," Blackie Holt said.

"Quit your worrying. Few Rangers have ever seen our faces. Besides, we are respectable bounty hunters doing the Rangers a favor by bringing Black Hawk to justice. Just continue to call me J.W. or Captain Dubose and I will call you Sergeant Hawkins. Why don't you go look at the wanted posters on the sheriff's office window? I need to know what my boys are up to these days!" Peal said. As Blackie walked away Peal scanned the busy street where a lone cowboy stood. Squinting his eyes, he recognized James Polk and quickly walked across the street. "Nice clothes, Peal. What are you up to?" James Polk asked.

"Just trying to make a living. I have a line on Black Hawk and have eyes out looking for him to cross the river. He is no good to me buried in the mountains of Mexico. You looking for a job?" Peal asked.

"Peal, you and I are looking for the same bird. The Hawk has some big money on his head. I know where he is hiding and you will probably end up in a Mexican prison if you go after him," Polk said.

"I am waiting for my boys to show up and we will decide. I have Blackie with me and that leaves me sort of out gunned. He is becoming more of a hindrance than a help," Peal said.

"Doing a job with your twins is the quickest way to get your name on a wanted poster. I think I will just wait and see what happens with the legislature. If they give Black Hawk a pardon the wanted poster money will disappear," Polk said.

"Word is it is a done deal. Bald Jo Kline will be coming into Texas to stand before the legislature anytime now. Meet me tonight in the livery and we will talk about it," Peal asked.

"No harm in listening," James Polk said.

Blackie made his way over to the sheriff's office and scanned through the list of names on the wanted list. The names of Jessie and Burl Peal had a straight line drawn through them as had several other outlaws on the list. The sheriff sat leaning against the wall of the jail with a toothpick in his mouth as Holt scanned the names.

"Hey sheriff, what means the names what have a line through them?" Holt asked.

"Who wants to know?" the sheriff asked.

The name's Hawkins. I rode with J. W. Dubose in the war. Surely you have heard of him?" Holt asked.

"Never heard of either one of you. You a bounty hunter or something?" the sheriff asked.

"A man's got to make a living!" Holt said.

"Well for your information those names that I have scratched out are no longer wanted by the law. They are now six feet under. The top three was hung by the hanging judge in Parker, Texas. The Peal twins drew down on Tindal Sloan and Jonathan Masters while trying to cut a herd," the sheriff said.

Blackie swallowed hard and took a deep breath. "The rest of these boys don't have much of a bounty on them. Not worth the trouble to hunt them down." The sheriff didn't bother to answer, and Blackie turned and walked away. He hated to tell Foster Peal what he had just learned.

Foster Peal sat in a rocking chair in front of the Texas House watching Blackie make his way through the slow-moving horses and wagons along the Texas side of Main Street. Blackie always had a nervous twitch and mumbled to himself when he had bad news to tell the captain. "Captain

Peal...err...I mean Captain Dubose...err...your boys must have been working for Longworth again. They were trying to cut a herd and was shot and killed by a couple of Texas Rangers, Tindall Sloan and Jonathan Masters. I would bet they were trying to make some easy money working for Longworth," Blackie stated.

Peal simmered for a long time. Grinding his teeth under his breath he muttered, "Longworth." A black mood came over him. Looking down the street at the railroad station he said. "We will start with the Rangers and then deal with Longworth. Blackie, stay here. I'm going to find out where Tindal Sloan was headed this morning. He and the other fellow must have bought a ticket."

"Captain, if we go after a Texas Ranger, you will have every Ranger and lawman in Texas looking for us!" Blackie said.

As if he had not heard a word Blackie had said, Peal rubbed his chin and spoke, "Sloan I have seen from a distance but this other feller Masters, I don't know."

A few minutes later Peal returned and said, "They boarded a train headed east the day they crossed the Rio Grande. The train is headed for Austin!"

"Forget the Rangers and let us just go down into Mexico and find Black Hawk. We can deal with Sloan after we get that big reward for Black Hawk. If we don't, someone else will beat us to the reward. Now that is a lot of money for just one man," Blackie said.

Peal's cold eyes fastened on Blackie, "They killed my boys, Blackie, and for that they will pay. The next train east will be leaving in a week. We will get our tickets and go see if we can get a line on the Don Verde," he said.

The following morning Foster Peal sat in the lobby of the Texas House. He suffered from a bad hangover and his day had started late. There had been no word of movement of Don Verde. Yawning deeply, he decided he needed to get breakfast before he headed for the station. A train pulled out of the station, and he watched it slowly disappear down the tracks picking up speed as it went. His drinking had made him careless and let a train through and he had not inquired if any businessmen were on the train. He would check on it after he got some food in him and get over this nauseous feeling. Maybe a nap after a good breakfast.

Hours later Captain Dubose straightened his best coat and stepped up on the rail station platform. He had shaved and bathed and cursed losing control as he had last night. "Good afternoon," he said with his best voice. He was about to speak when the telegrapher held up one finger something was coming over the wire and he was writing it down.

"Captain Dubose, I have been expecting to see you all morning. I even sent a runner but you were not in your room. We had a special come through this morning and it was the very train you seem to be inquiring about. There were several well-dressed men from the railroad main office and some Mexican as well as an American businessman. We have specials come through all the time headed for Austin. I was not alerted of this one until late," the telegrapher said.

"You got any names of people that were on this special?" Captain Dubose asked.

"Well, it only stopped to take on passengers and mail, but I did get a telegram after the train pulled out. It was addressed to a Mexican gentleman of some means, Señor Don J Verde. The telegram told him to return to Mexico and wait for word from Jonathan Masters as to when the meeting was rescheduled. To come now would not be prudent. Unfortunately, the special left before I could get the telegram to the gentlemen."

"Who signed that telegram," Foster Peal asked as sweetly as he could.

"Sir, this is like reading someone else's mail. But if you happen to look at this telegram while I am over getting pen and paper you would see," the telegrapher replied.

211

When the telegrapher returned Foster Peal was gone and so was the telegram.

Crossing the busy road Foster Peal's jaw was set hard. The special would make no other stops until it reached Austin. Busting into the room he was fuming. "Get up, Blackie! We just missed Black Hawk. A special came through while we were sleeping one off and guess who was on the train? Now, what would Tindal Sloan and Jonathan Masters be doing with Black Hawk?"

Blackie Holt rolled off the bed and retched his guts out.

"Blackie, sometimes you just simply disgust me. When you get yourself straight, I will be sitting in the main room trying to figure out how to get to Austin in less than a week. It seems our friend James Polk got on the special and left us behind," he growled.

ααααααα

For the past three weeks, Erlinda had been assisting Dr. Horace Lacy in some very delicate surgeries. This morning he stood beside her while she opened the patient and reassured her as she performed a very intricate operation. Slowly and skillfully, she removed a large mass that was causing the patient much discomfort.

"Now, Doctor, that was a very skillful piece of work with very little bleeding. Now close the incision and we are all done," Dr. Lacy said as he turned to the gallery above the operating table and asked if anyone had any questions. It was late evening, and the students were tired. All they wanted to do was leave campus and relax for the weekend.

"Erlinda, I wish we could spend more time here in surgery but tomorrow my wife and I will be heading for Austin. We received a telegram a few days ago. Our son is headed for Austin and wants us to meet him there," Horace said.

"Then we must travel together! It would give me more time to quiz you about some procedures I have heard that you have performed. My home is in Austin," she said.

"Well then, we might be able to spend some time together while we are in Austin," Horace said.

Erlinda chuckled, "My home is a railroad coach. It is parked on a siding in Austin. My father was an engineer for the railroad, and it was specially set up for him to live in. I loved it when I was little, and we would travel across the country. So, before he died, he made sure the rail car was my own special home and I could travel anywhere the rails would take me. I set up a clinic in one end of the car. Before I finished med school, I had helped people

213

up and down the line. Dad was impressed and saw that I needed nothing."

"A clinic on wheels that travels all over the country. Now, that is a novel idea, Erlinda. I am thoroughly impressed and anxious to see your clinic. My wife and I will be looking forward to traveling with you," Dr. Lacy said.

"I am anxious to meet your wife and son," Erlinda said.

'We are anxious to see our son. He has been on a cattle drive for most of a year bringing a special breed of cattle down from Canada. I feel he will follow me in the medical field. He needed a break from his studies, and this was a way to test himself and his grit. Giving him the room to develop on his own what he could not get at my side so, with much daily prayer, I sent him away," he said.

"Didn't you worry about your son in the wilds? There are many dangers in the wilderness, but some people seem to just fit in!" Erlinda blurted out.

The inquisitive look on her face and the way she blurted it out gave Dr. Lacy pause to wonder what she was thinking. She realized she was somewhat forward and said, "Well, we leave for the Texas Gulf Coast tomorrow and I must go get my bags packed. I will see you tomorrow morning on the Spirit of New Orleans. It is always prompt in leaving the dock," Erlinda said.

After she left, Dr. Lacy sat alone in the operating room. Above him, the gallery was empty of students. Horace began to think, *'Something just did not seem right. In the past, he had had so many encounters with people who had an ulterior motive that led to what was on their minds concerning his son having the blood of Black Hawk flowing through his veins. Truly the doctor had come to New Orleans to study under his team's leadership concerning invasive surgeries but there was something more. Could she possibly know that his son was the son of Bald Jo Kline, the famous Black Hawk?'* Dr. Lacy made no bones about confirming Calvin as his son in every way to anyone who asked. Horace hoped that Calvin would follow him in the medical field, but he was a man now and must make up his own mind. He would make sure Calvin had the best medical education that was possible.

Promptly at six, the whistle of the Spirit of New Orleans blew a long and piercing blast, and the gangway was swung away from the deck of the heavily ladened boat. Dr. Lacy retrieved their luggage from the hallway where the porter had left them, and Samantha started unpacking the dresses she had bought for the trip. "Well, we are underway. Let's go to the dining hall and have breakfast," Dr. Lacy said.

"You will not have to ask me twice!" Samantha said, laying aside the dress she was holding up in front of a mirror.

As the two walked along the side of the ship, each in their own thoughts, Samantha wondered if her son would have been changed from his experiences in the wilderness. Neither could know what Cal had faced in the wilderness where a person's life can be changed or ended in a moment of time.

The first person they spotted when they entered the dining hall was Erlinda. She was sitting alone at a large round table across the hall. Making their way across the room, Dr. Lacy introduced the two women. They had a cordial breakfast and sat drinking coffee as the boat lumbered across the rough gulf like a 200-pound ballerina.

The captain joined them for a quick introduction. It was shaping up to be a very busy day for him. "Erlinda, I see you have met Dr. Lacy and his wife Samantha. Good, good, good! I see you are not in the company of your daughter Isabella with you this trip." Without giving anyone a word, he added, "Dr. Lacy, I have enjoyed Erlinda and Isabella traveling the gulf with me on numerous occasions. Well, there are details that await my attention after a week in port. I hope you have a pleasant voyage." With that said he turned and left at a fast pace.

"Erlinda, I didn't know you were married," Horace blurted out.

"There is only my daughter and my house maid who is taking care of my daughter for this medical business trip I needed to make," Erlinda said.

"Business trip means working with me, I presume. I guess you lost your husband in the war?" Dr. Lacy asked.

Samantha gave him a shut-up look and Horace then noticed Erlinda's withdrawn appearance. Quietly he asked the waiter for a refill. Many thoughts were running through his head, but he managed to change the subject. "Well, I think I will take a walk along the ship and watch the shoreline. If you two will excuse me?"

Before Samantha could say anymore, Erlinda started talking, "My daughter is the world to me. She is thirteen and very tall for her age. She is so pretty she turns every head we pass. Isabella will be finishing up her studies this year in an all-girl school. I have her enrolled in the medical school in New Orleans. She is very young, but I will be there to help her along. My aunt lives not far from the school and will be able to look in on her when I am busy with my medical practice. I have no plans of my own except to further my medical abilities by working with fine doctors like your husband. So, tell me about your son," Erlinda said.

"Calvin is not too much older than your Isabella. He has finished most of his schooling and we did much the same as formal education. Now we hope he wants to follow his father in the medical field. When Cal graduated from college, Horace set him up to go on a cattle drive. He is gifted and very smart. He must only choose which school he wants to start his medical training in. Horace wanted him to experience the west firsthand. I have not heard from him for months and when we got the telegram, we were beside ourselves with joy!" Samantha Lacy said.

Erlinda sat for a moment wanting to speak, then said, "Samantha, I think I will go to my room and rest for a while. Tell Dr. Lacy I will see you both for lunch around noon if that is fine with you." With that said, she got up and dismissed herself.

C21 – Hard Explanations

Jonathan Masters drummed his fingers against the tabletop and considered the pardon that was beautifully printed on the paper with Jo Kline's name printed in bold letters and Black Hawk in the first sentence. It had been brought to Jonathan at his request. Jonathan worried once the word got out a pardon for Black Hawk had been approved that all hell would break out. He rolled the pardon up and slid it back into the protective sleeve. Looking at the other two, he pushed the sleeve across the table to Cal. "Gentlemen, I fear that allowing this to just slowly and quietly be made known will be presented to the public in a wrong way. It will cause a big stir here in Austin. I am glad we hold the official document in our hands with all the signatures affixed. There will be many who will try and back out of this," Jonathan Masters said.

"Now we are about to have to deal with Calvin's mother and father. It would have been better if you had not had them meet you here in Austin. How do you plan to do that?" Tindal Sloan asked.

"I don't intend to address the problem. I could not explain the situation. I intend to let Professor Jonathan Masters here do all the explaining. He has had years of pain and regrets from his dealings with my biological father. I have only had to deal with people that knew me as his blood son. Professor Masters had far greater reason to hate my father than I do. He decided to forgive him and has been the one most responsible for getting Black Hawk a pardon," Cal said.

"Well, I kind of knew that was coming. We have another problem. I suggest that when we walk down the street, we keep our eyes open to what is happening around us. Cal, you are a foot taller than most of the people here in Austin. It is highly likely that there are people here that may have seen Black Hawk and you are a spitting image of your biological father. We need to dress you like an easterner and get you out of those western clothes. That will help a lot," Jonathan Masters said.

Tindal Sloan looked across the street at the railroad station and said, "All the more reason I need to get a telegraph off and try and stop Don Jo Verde from leaving Mexico. He might walk into a hornet's nest and his appearance will start the mob action. Pointing at the station, Tin said, "I will get that taken care of right now."

"Be discrete, Tindal. It will be read by every telegrapher along the lines," Jonathan replied.

"Jonathan, pin your badge where it can be always seen. Then they will not notice the boy walking with you," Sloan suggested.

"We are headed for that store over there so I can dress this rugged cowpoke like a gentleman and scholar from Rhode Island," Jonathan said.

Days later, sitting on the boardwalk of the hotel, Captain Dubose sat watching as people walked along the street. It had taken him a week to get to Austin, yet he had not seen anyone that remotely resembled Black Hawk. Peal was enjoying the evening breeze and the assortment of people that came riding by. He had especially enjoyed the odd tall lanky man wearing a top hat, riding a tall mule, and surrounded by four fine Bloodhounds, the kind he had seen in New Orleans. The other two men riding with him were not hard to figure out. One was Tindal Sloan and the other was the spitting image of Black Hawk except about eighteen years too young. He had to be the Hawk's son. *'This was getting more interesting by the day,'* he thought. Twitching his nose, he looked around at Blackie who had come up behind him. "Sergeant, it's time for your weekly bath. See that bathhouse down the street?"

Blackie's head turned slightly and grunted, "Yes."

"Go down there and get yourself cleaned up and git rid of that scraggly beard. Consider that an order. Take all the time you need and come back presentable," Peal ordered.

Hours later he smiled to himself. Down the boardwalk came two women followed by two porters carrying their luggage. Samantha and Erlinda were dressed in the latest fashions. Not far behind them, Dr. Lacy instructed the baggage clerk where the luggage was to be taken. The trip across the Gulf had been uneventful and Dr. Lacy had caught up on some much-needed rest on a deck chair aboard the Spirit of New Orleans. Then the train ride had taken them from the coast to Austin. Nothing more had been said of Erlinda's daughter and Samantha was too proper to pry into something Erlinda did not want to pursue.

The Cattleman's Palace was a grand hotel with all the comforts one would want. While Dr. Lacy checked in at the desk, Samantha asked if her son was staying in this hotel. "My son's name is Calvin Lacy and…"

"Oh yes, madam! Your son is a well-mannered gentleman and I think he is in his room now. That will be room number five just down the corridor and on the left. He is with a gentleman who is well known here in Texas, Ranger Tindal Sloan," the clerk said.

"Come, Erlinda! Let me introduce you to my son!" Samantha said. In just a moment she was knocking on the door number five.

"Who is it?" came a throaty voice from the room just before the door was opened by a tall lanky man with a gun in one hand and a razor in the other. His face covered with shaving cream. "Sorry, ladies. I was expecting the porter," Tin Sloan said.

"I am looking for my son. He is supposed to be in this room," Samantha said.

"Mom, is that you?" Cal asked hearing the familiar voice in the hall.

"It is your mother, Calvin!" Samantha was almost beside herself. Her prayers for his safety through all these months had been answered.

Suddenly in the dimly lit hall a tall, browned from the sun, Calvin Lacy stood. The spitting image of his father except for a very gentle and youthful smile. Months in a wilderness land had changed her son. Samantha Lacy was suddenly taken back by the resemblance to Black Hawk she had blocked from her mind in his youthful years.

Behind her, Erlinda saw the man before her for the first time and muttered the words "Black Hawk" before she caught herself.

Calvin Lacy heard Erlinda mutter the name Black Hawk and he turned to her with a smile. "I do not believe we've met! Calvin Lacy is my name. I am Calvin Lacy, son of Dr. Horace and Samantha Lacy. Hello, Mother! Did you miss me?" Calvin said all in one breath.

Samantha was taken aback with the reply Calvin had given to Erlinda and his appearance but quickly changed the subject. Putting her hands on her hips and faking a frown she exclaimed. "Calvin Lacy, you have grown up in the wilderness, and I simply will not allow you to do so before you are old enough to shave." The two hugged and Samantha wiped away tears of gladness and said, "Yes, son, we have missed you! Your father sat many a night by the fireplace mulling over whether he had done the right thing. Welcome back!"

Erlinda stood by the two, her head down. Shamed by her outburst and for not leveling with Dr. Lacy and Samantha from the start. "Samantha, I am so sorry for my outburst and feel I owe you an explanation," she said.

"Pay it no mind! We will have plenty of time to talk," Samantha said.

Dr. Lacy came walking down the hall with Jonathan Masters.

"Cal, I see you have made it back. It is good to see you son," Horace said his eyes going from his son to the tall, lanky Tindal Sloan.

"I declare son! How in the world did you end up with Professor Masters? What are you doing here, Jonathan?" Samantha exclaimed.

Before Jonathan could answer, Cal said, "It is a long story, Mother. Why don't we all get a table in the dining room before we start discussing my galivanting all over the countryside. I have not had a good meal since we left Mexico. Professor Masters can answer all your questions," Cal said with a mischievous grin.

"Mexico? You were supposed to be driving cattle down from Canada. What pray-tell were you doing down in Mexico?" Samantha asked.

At the end of the dark hall, a door had been slightly opened and Blackie Holt had heard the entire conversation. He had to keep this straight and make sure he relayed it to Foster Peal correctly. It was a lot to remember, and Peal would ask a lot of questions.

A few minutes later, Blackie came down the street mumbling to himself and trying to remember everything he had heard in the darkened hall. "Foster, I did as you told me. I went to the bathhouse and got myself all cleaned up. When I left there, I headed back to the room, and low and behold, there stood a young Black Hawk. His mother was not too satisfied with the answers she was getting, and they all went to the dining room to have lunch and discuss the boy's goings and comings," Blackie said.

"Then so shall we! We must find a table close enough that we can overhear their conversations," Foster said.

Foster, I do not think that is a good idea," Blackie said.

"Blackie, just let me do the thinking," Foster said.

Jonathan sat at the end of the big table and considered what he would say. Not coming up with a satisfactory way of explaining the last year for several people's lives at one time, he said, "Any explanation will not be easy, Samantha, but we definitely have a lot to tell you."

To make it move along a little faster, Erlinda decided to speak. "Professor Masters, you three were in Mexico. Were you by any chance in a small town called Paso Verde? How and why were you there?" she asked.

"Well," Jonathan said pulling out the plate and unwrapping it, "this is part of the reason. I found this plate in the saddle bag of one of the Peal twins. It looked so much like Cal he had to explain it was not him on the plate," he said. Then starting at the cattle drive he explained what had happened in the last year. "We found Cal leading a cattle drive down from Canada. Rustlers were set to take the herd when we found him. With our help, the trail boss was able to stop the rustlers from taking his herd. Then we headed for Mexico," Jonathan said

The plate got passed around until it reached Samantha. "This surely is my son and his horse's picture. I do not understand!" she said.

"That is not me, Mother! That is Black Hawk! Now you know the awkward position I have been put in because of my looks," Cal said.

"Is that why you are dressed in those ridiculous clothes? Jonathan, only an easterner would wear that hat which would surely get Cal in a fight in this part of the West!" Samantha said chidingly.

Cal took off his derby and looked around at Professor Masters grinning. "I do not think your scheme is working, Professor. We may have made matters worse," Cal said.

Dr. Erlinda McAllen had not said anything. Her exasperation was finally getting to her, and she interrupted the conversation. "I must speak!" was all she said, and the entire table became quiet. "First, Dr. Lacy, it was no accident I was your assistant for the past few months. I have an urgent need and I am sure the only one who can help me is you. You have dealt with the Snow wagon train massacre and bringing your wife back to a normalcy over all these years." Stopping for a minute she took a deep breath and looked around the table. "I have had to face it alone. No one was there to help me when I gave birth to Black Hawk's child. No one has been there for me in any way. I have dealt with all the hurt and sorrow dealing with my child. She was not accepted among other children. It was soon known she was the offspring of the infamous Bald Jo Kline. She is thirteen now and on a day-to-day basis, I must deal with depression and heartache, and fear that she might harm herself. That is why I came to you in New Orleans. I desperately need your help."

"Erlinda, we will work together. I would like to meet her soon," Dr. Lacy said.

Erlinda continued, "Isabella was doing well and looking forward to a trip to the mountains. We always take a yearly trip into the mountains of Mexico where my mother was born. It helps my daughter to relax and smile for a brief time. It was a pleasant time until this last fateful trip when the very reason for all the sorrow and bitterness I have dealt with was there. Black Hawk was present there. He was no longer a raging painted warrior that woke me in fear each night. Instead a kind man who spoke Spanish and English properly and showed a high degree of intelligence. Now Doctor, I need you to help me with my daughter and my own bitterness. I fear for her life if she cannot come to grips with this situation. I cannot find a way to get her back to reality and sometimes she falls into a deep dark depression I cannot understand. Yes, like your Samantha's son, my daughter is the offspring of an attack on me by Black Hawk thirteen years ago," she said.

In the next room separated by only a thin wall, Foster Peal and Blackie Holt listened as the story of Bald Jo Kline, the Black Hawk unfolded. He learned that Black Hawk's child was a girl outside of town in a railroad car protected by an aged maid. Somewhere in town Black Hawk was not far away. He would be brought forth when he was to appear in front of the legislative body and governor.

"Originally our intention was to find Bald Jo Kline and bring him back to Texas for trial. What we found was not in the least what we expected," Professor Masters said.

Cal first explained coming face to face with Black Hawk and how Kline found out the man before him was the papoose he had traded for three bottles of whisky. Shortly after that, Black Hawk left the Indian nation and their way of life. He ended up in New Orleans where he came person to person with the woman he had taken from the Snow wagon train.

"Black Hawk had gone to Mexico and while traveling in the mountains came across an impoverished town on the verge of extinction. Held together only by a blacksmith preacher whose former life was riding with the Comancheros and Apache. The change Jo Kline made was so profound. The whole town knew they had been saved by the influence of one man who called himself Sir Don Jo Verde. He saved the town from a raid by Comancheros and brought life to the town. They honored the man with a Don Jo Verde Day. The town painted a full wall-size mural at the local gathering place and on plates. The most amazing thing was the most feared and hated Indian had been converted by reading the Bible in order to learn to speak English," Jonathan Masters said.

"I do not believe it. The man who caused me so much hurt and pain has become a Christian and my son knows him personally. I refuse to hear any more of this!" Samantha said and left the table for her room.

Dr. Lacy rose from his seat and watched his wife leave the dining room. "Jonathan, you have talked to this man and believe all he says is true? After what he had done to you and your beloved Elizabeth? How is this possible? Professor Masters, you have gone mad!" Dr. Lacy said in pure astonishment.

Erlinda sat quietly trying to cope with all the heartache that had resurfaced again. All sitting around the table lapsed into silence for a long minute then Erlinda sighed and stated, "Dr. Lacy, all that has been said here is true."

Dr. Lacy turned to his son and said, "Son, you know all the hurt your mother has been through because of that monster."

"I do, Father. I am a product of that man's evil ways. I share her hurt. Please excuse me as I want to talk with Mother," Cal said and left the table.

C22 – Old Memories

While Jonathan and Dr. Lacy conversed with Erlinda, Tin Sloan excused himself from the table and took a stroll down the main street of Austin. It was a busy day and the streets were filled with people. After visiting a saddle shop, Tin walked along the boardwalk. Suddenly, a loud laughter caught his attention, and he stopped outside the swinging doors of the saloon. Lowering his head, he breathed deeply and waited to hear that voice again. He knew that laugh and it brought a frown to his face. Turning, he walked through the swinging doors to see if his ears had deceived him. The strong smell of weak beer and cigar smoke was one he could never get used to. It had been a year since he had seen Olive Shingle and the sight of her gave him a down cast feeling in the pit of his stomach. Olive was working her way through the crowded saloon stopping at each table and laughing loudly with the men sitting there. A typical barroom woman, now she held little resemblance to the Olive he had known growing up. With deep disappointment showing on his face, he turned and reached for the swinging doors. Over the years, he had made it a point to keep tabs on her, but this was a development he had hoped he would never see. Olive had been his childhood sweetheart. Now years later it had come to this. It did not surprise him because each time he had seen her, she had been in a lower state of affairs than the last. Tin had tried to reason with her over the years, but there was never a time when Olive would listen to anyone. For a moment, he stood trying to decide if he should even talk to her. He realized it would have been a waste of time. She had lost her once innocent look to a hard face. Just as he started to make his way out of the swinging doors, he heard his name called from across the saloon.

"Tindal Sloan, wait!" Olive shouted almost in a state of alarm. Quickly, she made her way across the crowded saloon and grabbed his arm as if to make sure he did not run away. "Were you going to just walk away and not say hello?" Olive asked.

"It had crossed my mind," Tindal said.

"How did you find me in Austin. I have only been here a week," Olive said.

"I was not looking for you. You know I am a Ranger and spend a lot of time here in Austin," Tin said.

"Maybe I was looking for you," Olive said.

"Last I heard you were in Oklahoma. What brought you back?" Tin inquired.

"I came back on the stage. Maybe I will just go back to Lubbock," Olive said.

"Olive, you know Lubbock is not a good town for you. You should have stayed in Oklahoma," Tin said.

"The sheriff had different ideas for me so, before I ended up in jail, I got on the coach and headed south," she said sarcastically.

"Olive, you are doing just as always, keeping bad company. I gave up hope for you a long time ago. Only time will erase the feelings I have for you. With that said I will be on my way. You will not be happy there in Oklahoma, or anywhere else for that matter. You and I have come a long way only in different directions," Tin said.

"Tindal, wait!" Olive called as he strolled off down the boardwalk. In a huff, Olive Shingle turned and went back into the saloon.

Tindal Sloan was not the only one who had heard his name called out in the saloon. Sitting at a card table, two of the Sellers gang were playing cards. As soon as they heard Sloan's name and saw Olive rushing out the saloon door, they made a quick exit out the rear door.

Hasty Fletcher wiped his hat band and looked at John Allen Murphy. "That was a close call. Tindal Sloan must be tracking us to be here in Austin," one said. From the alley someone said, "Sloan is not following you two boneheads. He has

Black Hawk stashed somewhere out around here. Word is he has gotten that Indian a pardon from the governor." From the dark alley walked James Polk smiling at the two. "Of all the places to come after a job, why did you idiots come to Austin? Get smart and get out of town or you might get locked up for cheating at cards. Then Tin Sloan will simply deliver you two to Judge William Self in Parker for your hanging," James Polk said.

"James is right. You go to the livery and get our horses. Sloan had never seen you, but he knows me. I will stay back here behind the saloon. I want to let Olive know we are leaving," he said.

"Are you crazy? Forget about Olive! I want to get as far from Austin as I can get. Sellers was right! We needed to lay low in Matamoras for a month or so. There are too many Rangers here in Austin. We hang around here and get drunk, we will end up in jail. Sloan knows me if he sees me, we will be the guest at a hanging," John Allen responded.

"You two head for Matamoras and I will ketch up with you in a week or so. I am working a deal. If it falls through, we will meet Sellers in Mexico. He is lining up a bank east of here," James Polk said.

"Just give me a minute, John Allen. You get our horses," Hasty said.

Captain J. W. Dubose (Foster Peal) sat inside the saloon at a corner table.

Across the table from him a dark dapper gentlemen watched the man across from him. "Where are those two boys of yours that I met last we saw each other," the man asked.

"You see the man the girl was calling to at the saloon doors?" Foster asked.

The man turned and squinted his eyes from under the costly hat he was wearing. "I see a man with a star!" he replied.

"That man is a Texas Ranger. His name is Tindall Sloan. He and another Ranger killed my boys in a gun battle. I fully intend to kill him when I kill Black Hawk," Foster Peal said.

"You and I have an agreement! If you do anything to bring notoriety to yourself, our deal will be off. Do as I asked, and you can return and take care of your vendetta later. You leave Black Hawk and the Ranger alone until I give you permission to kill him," the dark man said.

Foster Peal bristled under his collar but after a few minutes he smiled and nodded a "yes." "Our business arrangements are more important than personal matters now," he said.

The man rose and left the saloon, saying, "Very good. Now, I must be about my banking business and will expect to see you soon."

Peal watched the man walk by the Ranger and the barmaid leaving while

Sloan and Olive were talking. He had been waiting patiently for Blackie to return from his errand. Somewhere around the city of Austin, there was a rail car that held the daughter of Black Hawk. If Blackie found the rail car, it would be easy enough to get the girl. Then there is the matter of Tin Sloan to deal with. His boys were dead, and Sloan had to pay for that. James Polk made his way in the back door and spotted Peal sitting against the wall. "Where is Blackie?" Polk asked.

Foster shook his head in exasperation. "Blackie is an extra burden for me these days," he said.

The morning broke without a cloud in the sky. Along the tracks behind the city of Austin, Dr. Erlinda's railcar sat. It would be a hot day, but the coach was positioned between two hills that shaded the railcar morning and evening. Only the midday hours were hot in the coach. Austin was a special town where the lady doctor and Isabella could get lost in the busy streets. Occasionally, the wandering spirit would hit Erlinda and the two would again feel the swaying of the coach as it headed down the ribbons of steel. There was something about the constant swaying that soothed Isabella. She loved to stand on the back platform and sway with the rail car movement and whistle the beautiful melodies that came across her young mind. The movement of the coach had been a poultice for both as it moved toward the setting or rising of the sun.

In the grand hotel in Austin, Erlinda rolled over and looked at the sun rising out of the east. She had stayed in the hotel to have a talk with Dr. Lacy and this morning she would ride out with the Ranger and Calvin Lacy to confront Black Hawk. This time she would get answers to nagging questions and settle the matter in her mind. Deep in the feather bed, her eyes peered into the darkness deep in thought, *'How was it possible, if God really cared, would He allow the reason for her hate and fears to show up in the very town her mother had been born in? He even claimed the town's name for his own and helped the people there to claim a real existence which seemed to be a stumbling point in her life. No matter the help he had been to the people stuck in poverty.'*

The day before, Isabella had grown tired of the coach and wanted to go to Austin where her mother was. There she could lay across the bed and watch the people move about the city. The hot summer months were coming and were not to her liking. She looked forward to getting enrolled in school. The sooner the better. She would meet some friends that would accept her. Long before noon, she was walking along the tracks with her little dog, Peppy.

Coming in the opposite direction with his head down, Blackie Holt mumbled to himself. He did not like the way Peal was thinking. Messing with a young girl, even the daughter of Black Hawk, would lead to the hangman. He quickly loosened the scarf around his neck and swallowed hard.

Suddenly, barking at his feet and annoying him was the girl's little dog. Looking up he saw the girl standing right in front of him. His horse had been the first to see the dog and had jerked back on the reins. Not having a good grip Blackie found himself watching his horse running away being chased by the small dog. As he looked, back the girl had turned and was almost back to the coach. Now he had a long hot walk back to the hotel.

Walking up on the boardwalk, Blackie stood by Foster Peal. Peal sat in a rocking chair his feet on the banister in front of him. "Blackie, why are you covered with dirt and sweating like a pig?" Peal asked.

"My horse ran away, and I had to walk halfway around Austin to get back here. I found the girl," he said.

"Well done, Blackie! Now, all we have to do is find the Black Hawk. That should not be too hard. I have watched Sloan ride out every morning and I suspect he is headed out to meet with him. When we find Black Hawk, we will have the leverage to get him to do anything we need him to do. Time for your weekly visit to the bathhouse," Peal said.

"Peal, we better not mess with the girl. If we do, we are going to be hung for sure. What good is finding Black Hawk? From what we have heard he is a free man with no bounty on his head," Blackie said.

"Just go find me James Polk would you, Blackie? Just do that one thing without giving me a lot of your talk. You two come back here sober," Peal said. *'The price on Black Hawk's head has no meaning for me,'* Peal thought.

Early the next morning Peal, Polk, and Blackie were up long before dawn. It took only a few minutes to get their mounts saddled and make their way out of the city of Austin.

Tindal was a creature of habit. This morning however he had company on his trip to see Black Hawk. Erlinda and Calvin were with him on this trip out of town. They rode for hours following three sets of horse prints that were made earlier that morning. Not long after daylight, Tin called a halt while he mentally took in the prints of the three horse's hooves.

"What are you looking for?" Cal asked.

"Most every morning I leave town the same way," Tindal said. "Usually, I leave at the same time. I am easy to figure, but I am also cautious. Every morning I have been watched leaving town by one individual that sits in a rocker on the hotel porch. This morning he was not there. I recognized the hoof prints of one of the horses. He is a gelding belonging to a bank robber by the name of James Polk. When we get back to Austin, I will watch the livery. I might get lucky and get one of the Sweetwater Bank Robbers right here in Austin. I will also know who rides with him by these other prints," Tin said.

A mile further, the prints they had been following turned off onto a rocky path that led into the hills where there were good views of the road. Tin and Cal both got down from their horses and again examined the hoof prints. Each made mental notes and continued to the meeting place where they were to meet Black Hawk.

James Polk lowered his binoculars and swallowed hard. "Peal, Tin Sloan is tracking us. He knows my horse. Of that, I am sure. That means he will be looking for me in Austin. You boys are on your own. I am leaving as fast as my horse will get me away from Austin," Polk said.

"Wait a minute! Don't you want your share of the Black Hawk bounty?" Peal said.

"I should have left last night like Fletcher and Murphy. If Black Hawk is no longer wanted, the reward will no longer be valid. See you boys later," James Polk got on his horse and rode away.

C23 – Broken Reasoning

It was early, and the three rode along in silence, each in his own thoughts. Cal noticed Erlinda took side looks at him several times. So, after a while, Cal slowed his horse. "Dr. Erlinda, tell me about your daughter. I would like to meet her. It seems from what I have heard she is having a hard time coping with the knowledge of her biological father. At her age, I was pretty much in the same frame of mind. Maybe having a big brother will help her size things up better," Cal stated earnestly.

Erlinda came out of her thoughtful mode and suddenly smiled. "Cal, you are right! I have been looking to the wrong ones for help with Isabella. You are her blood brother, and in you, she will know someone who is living the same experiences. As soon as we get back to town, I would like to introduce you to her," Erlinda said.

From a hill, a far distance from Tindal, Cal, and Erlinda, Black Hawk raised his binoculars back to his eyes. Scanning away from the approaching riders, he focused on three men lying on a hill watching the road. "Pablo, they seem to be interested in the riders coming down the road," Señor Jo Verde said.

"There is a stagecoach that travels this road every morning. They could be highwaymen waiting to rob it," Pablo said. Pablo lowered his binoculars and spoke, "Señor, these three look to be bounty hunters. Surely, they watch the good doctor and especially the lawman with the star. From this distance, I cannot be sure, but I think I have seen one of these hombres before."

"They have allowed the three riders to pass. I will head back to the settlement to greet the doctor and my son. If they move, that means they are tracking my friends. Now, what do you think they are following them for?" Don Jo Verde asked.

"They are bounty hunters following the lawman to find you. They want the bounty. Señor Don Verde, we must go back to Mexico. We do not need to be here. I fear for your safety," Pablo said.

"Not just yet, my friend. We must meet with the people who have given me a purpose to live as a free man. Now we must go. I want to be in camp when they arrive," Jo Verde said.

Señor Don Verde was waiting for the three as they rode through the small group of settlers. The railroad passes through this country and has left a trading post surrounded by wagons and tents. People moving west were camped alongside a fast-moving stream. The tent city grew with each passing train. There were several different Indian tribes represented as well as traveling settlers.

Each day, Jo would stop and converse with an Indian, or group of Indians, standing along the street or around the trading post. There were several saloons as well as a single church that had been built along the dusty street.

Jo stopped the party long enough to give instructions. "Pablo, you stay along the street and watch the saloons for the three we spotted watching the road. If they show up, try and get an idea of what they are up to," Don Verde said.

With a nod, Pablo moved his horse to the hitching rail.

At the end of the tent city, Señor Don Jo Verde stopped in front of a large tent. An elderly Spanish woman stepped and waited for her orders. He instructed her to serve his friends fresh bread and water when they arrived.

A train heading west sat blowing steam at the station as Ranger Tin Sloan and his party passed along the main street. It was not long until Tin Sloan rode to the tent followed by Erlinda and Calvin Lacy. Quickly the maid came out to follow the instructions she had received. "Thank you, Señorita. We will sit here in the shade for a while. If you would please prepare some lunch for my friends," Jo Verde stated.

It was obvious that the don was glad to see the three and especially glad to see Erlinda. He spoke politely to her first and offered her a seat. He gave Cal a polite nod and smiled. Then he took Tin Sloan by the hand and shook it warmly, and said, "I am glad to see you. I hope your ride was uneventful, but I must warn you that you were followed, or I might say stalked."

It was obvious the don was glad to see the woman doctor and his son. He spoke cordially to her. Treating them both with respect, but in both cases, he tried not to be overbearing. He realized he was the reason for most of the hurt in their lives.

Tin untied a package from behind his saddlebags and handed them to Araña. "Here are the things you needed. As for the three men, we followed their horse's tracks until they reached the fork in the road and figured they were in the boulders watching to see which way we were going," Tin said.

"The three were following you. One was well dressed. I could not tell if he was clean-shaven or had a light beard. One had dark hair and a beard. The third was a tall slender man with sandy hair and new jeans and a red bandana. My man Pablo is watching to see if they appear here. Hopefully he can find out what they are up to," the don said.

"The tall slender boy was James Polk. I recognized his horse's hoof prints," Tin said. He was not surprised that the Señor knew that his group had been followed. Men of the West always thought ahead of what may come their way. Instantly, Tin's mind was working. He always noticed how people were dressed or looked as he moved along the streets each day. If anyone person was seen too many times a day in his vicinity, it was likely Tin was being watched. Being a Ranger was an easy way to make enemies with the people he arrested or family members of the men he had to kill. "Sounds like bounty hunters. They are following me to find you," Tin said.

Changing the subject, Señor Don Verde turned to Erlinda, and said, "I was not expecting you, but I am very glad that you came. The first time we met, you left so quickly that I did not have a chance to beg your forgiveness. That meeting changed my life forever, and I know there is no way I can ever make up for the wrong I have done. I know you did not ever expect to see me. Now that you have, I would like to know if it is possible to ever make up for all the harm and earn your forgiveness. If I could take back the damage I have done, I would gladly do so. There is not a moment of my day I do not have regret cross my mind. I did not realize, as an Indian, I would someday have this change of heart. I do not know what else to say, but I am glad you came."

Erlinda stood for a long time staring at the man who had changed her life so many years before. Behind her Don Verde caught the eye of three men who had come and stood just out of hearing. "Please excuse me for a minute," Jo said and walked away before she could say anything.

Two of the men were Indians who were dressed in the Comanche apparel and the other was a small wiry Mexican with a hard look. For the next few minutes, they talked in low tones, and then Jo turned and beckoned Araña to come. A discussion in Spanish was continued, and Araña shook his head and left with the three men. Jo returned to his guest who sat in an open tent shade where the old Spanish woman was serving them cool water and pastries. Trying not to be too cordial, Jo addressed Erlinda once again. "You came a long ride from Austin! Dr. Lady, you must have come here to see me for some reason. Please speak freely! What is on your mind?" he asked.

Erlinda took a deep breath and looked at the other two before starting. "Just to let you know, I have refused to medically treat any Indians that come to me for help. I have lived my life with hate for you and anyone else that is of Indian descent. It may be too late for me to live any other way. I was a good and proper person with a desire to help the lower class of people that surrounded me. I now have no place in my life for the God that would allow me and my family to have been treated in such a manner. My life was all planned out. I could have achieved much more than I have, but because of your attack on that horrible day, people now look down on me. I am a common woman. The mother of a half-breed. I would have rather known that you were still out in the wilderness living the life of an Indian," she stated.

Erlinda continued "For years, I have hoped I would hear of your death by the very means you have lived. I was comfortable waiting for that end. Instead, you show up in the very town my mother was born in living your life as a noble person, a Don, well respected and loved by all. At no time have I ever received such acclamations from the very people that needed my services. You had given them purpose and hope. You had shown them they were not helpless. They had skills that I should have recognized. The very person that I hated has been elevated from a savage to a person of intelligence. I did not recognize you at first but then a cold realization of who you were sent chills over me. I tried to hide it from Isabella. Somehow, she figured it out and her depression became much worse. I do not know how I feel now. It is like I lived long ago in another world. If I said I forgive you, it would be a lie."

Jo Verde was taken aback and sat for a moment thinking of what response he should give. "You came here with a lot on your heart." He removed his sombrero, rolled up the sleeve of his white shirt, cleared his throat, then said, "I must speak freely, or my silence may cause your heart to hate me even more. It would possibly distance you from our Creator who hears all and remembers all. First, I must wonder if you have ever given any consideration to God before or after the raid. Only you and He know the answer to that. I must not allow my silence to cause sin to further damage your heart. I learned to hate from the other end of society. You hate looking down. I hated looking up. The problem for both of us is that you were happy with what you had with no need to change. You would have continued looking down at those beneath you and having pity. I was happy living wild and free, not having to answer to anyone. My strength and cunning made me superior to those around me that I lorded my will over. If you do not change, you will perish in a place called hell. Ironically, I have found the Lord of Lords and King of Kings and have submitted my heart to His Will. Is it not ironic there may come a day when you will look up from a place called hell and see me in the heaven? A place you thought you deserved for your goodness," he said.

Erlinda was dumbfounded. She was not expecting to hear such depth from one she had hated for the last thirteen years.

"When I was very young," he continued, "I lived on a large grassy plain in Africa. Our village was surrounded by a wooden stick fence. The sharpened sticks gave us the only protection that we had from wild animals that hunted in the night. One night my mother woke me with a frightened whisper and said in my ear, "Get up, Joseph! The Zulu come!"

We ran from our hut and joined the other villagers in a big grass hut in the center of our village. We huddled in the dark room in stark fear. I was old enough to know that the Zulu were our tribe's worst nightmare. They were coming to kill us. There was a White man in our village. He was called a missionary. He calmed us down with his prayers. All night he prayed and walked around the outside of the hut. We would see him passing the windows in the moonlight. Every so often, he would pass the window, and for some reason, I knew if I saw him pass while he was praying and holding his Bible aloft, we were safe. We heard the frightening yells of the painted men just out of our camp. It was a long and fearful night. The morning came, and the Zulu had left, never to return. Later we were captured by a Black slave trader and sold to a White man who took us to America where we were sold as slaves. I grew to hate while I was very young."

"A year later, I sat on the bottom step of a slave cabin bitterness in my heart for my position in life. My mother sat on the next step above me and hummed a tune. She wrapped her loving arms around me and asked, *'Son, why are you bitter? You should be glad you are here. There are no Zulu here. Bitterness can cause you to hate! Hate is a terrible sin. All things in life can be either good or bad but must work to make you a better man, or you yourself will become like the Zulu.'* Don Jo Verde held out his hands, palms down, and spoke, "Look at the skin on my hands and face. As a boy, I stood on an auction block in New Orleans and was sold. After that day, I never saw my mother again. My skin and strength put me on the bottom of a society where people with money bought and sold me like a mule to be used until I died."

"Two of the men who sold me were Black men. The only kindness I was shone in my life was by the White missionary and the Mexican Don who bought me and gave me my freedom. Later in life, I stood on the plains of America facing my own son." His eyes went over to connect with Cal's. "Suddenly, I realized I had become what I hated the most. My mother's words came back to me. *'Do not hate my son or you will become like the Zulu.'* I realized hate had made me a Zulu," the don concluded.

Erlinda shrugged, and it was plain she did not like what she was hearing.

Jo was no longer looking her in the eyes but cast a downward look between them.

Tindall Sloan was normally a quiet man and had said nothing. However, when the exchange died down, he said, "Doctor, we will wait to the cool of the evening, then ride back into town before dark."

Pablo eased his sombrero back over his head and turned to adjust his girth as the well-dressed man made his way down the main street of tent city. At a safe distance so as not to be detected, he watched as the two men rode past the tent where Don Jo Verde stood with his guests. There were many riders along the street and only Pablo and Tindal paid attention to the two.

"It's time for us to go back to town. I will get the horses while you two say goodbye," Tin said. A few minutes later the three left the tent city behind. For a while, all three were quiet; each in their own thoughts. Erlinda turned one time as they were leaving to see Don Jo Verde still watching the three riding along the road. "Pablo, you and the Comanche braves see to it that our friends arrive in Austin safely," Jo said. Pablo left and was soon joined by two hard-faced Comanche Indians. His head full of thoughts, Jo Verde walked away along the stream. It was an unusually warm day for this time of year. He wanted to return to his home. He was happy there with his books and friends he had grown to appreciate. Francis Littlefield was right. He needed to be back in Mexico. He felt he had not resolved any of the issues in his life. Maybe over time with silence from him, the old wounds he had created would start to heal.

ααααααα

After James Polk had left, Foster Peal's plan had fallen apart. Without the fast gun of Polk, he did not have the backing he needed. Depending on Blackie to go take the daughter of Black Hawk was not going to happen. It was always his style to stay in the background and let the younger, more careless boys of youth do his dirty work for him. In the past, the twins had been his way of getting his creative evil accomplished. Sending Blackie after the girl would end in failure, no doubt. He and Blackie entered Austin very early in the afternoon and went straight to the first saloon on the main street. He would start here.

Along the street, he made sure that the name Black Hawk was the main source of discussion. It took very little to get men to argue, and someone always had a tale of the brutality of the Black Hawk. As soon as the three entered Austin, Pablo turned the Comanche braves away and told them it would be better for them if they stayed away from Austin for a few days. Nodding, they raised their arms in peace and headed back to the tent settlement. Pablo went to

the closest cantina just in time to hear a
heated discussion concerning Black Hawk.
He did not linger. He had heard what was
beginning to fester. It was time to get back
to Don Jo Verde and let him know what
was being said.

Now dressed in his best suit, Foster
Peal became Captain J.W. Dubose.
Adjusting his New Orleans hat and
touching a match to his stogie, he walked
along the boardwalk. Now it was time to
do a little recruiting. The South at this time
had many men that were spoiling to back a
cause no matter the depth of evil. Getting
back on his horse, he rode along the main
street with a plan in mind. At the east end
of the main street were the cattle holding
pens. Usually, there were several hundred
head of cattle waiting for cattle cars to
arrive. A bar where the down and out of
Texas imbibed stood at that end of town.
Circling the saloon, he found an
abandoned blacksmith shop. There was a
good bale of hay leaning against the corner
of the building. "This will do," he said as
he and Blackie walked around the building.
On one rear corner of the barn, he found
an old well that was covered with rotten
boards. Riding around to the front of the
building they entered the swinging doors.
The captain looked out of place, but to
him, appearance was always a big part of
his schemes. Every head turned as he
entered the building. It was not long until a

big man made his way over to the table. The captain noticed the smell before he came to stand by the table. This man made Blackie smell good on the worst day of Texas heat.

"Hey, feller! You come down to buy cattle or sell them?" he asked gruffly.

Foster Peal looked up at the man and considered the possibilities, and said, "Neither, my good man. I am looking for a few men seeking employment."

"What kind of job you got and how much does it pay?" came the response.

The captain studied the man. Letting the man see he was considering if he had the grit that the job required.

"I will need three men. Men who do not mind stepping over the line if the pay is right," the captain said.

"Three men, huh? I know a couple who will do most anything for good silver. We don't take no paper money, you see," the man said pulling up a chair and sitting down.

"You pick your men. Don't pick any who are opposed to shedding a little blood. If this is interesting to you, here are four silver dollars. You and your men go over to that bath house. Get yourselves a bath and some new clothes. Meet me tonight in the barn back of this place. Stay sober! I smell liquor on any one of you, and the deal is off," Foster Peal said.

"Say, I don't even know your name," the big man said.

"I did not ask for your name. You do not need to know mine," Peal said. Rising from the table Peal and Holt left the bar.

"Foster, you just gave that trash more money than he has seen in a month. We will not see hide nor hair of him or his friends," Blackie said.

Before the sun went down Blackie and Peal approached the barn. Peal stayed a short distance away with his horse hidden. Blackie entered the back of the barn and climbed up the rickety ladder to the loft. Laying in the loft on a couple of bales of old hay he thought of the mess he was in. Long before the meeting time, the three showed up and entered the barn.

"Morris, so far I like this plan. I haven't had a clean pair of clothes in a year. This feller must be carrying a bundle. I say I stick a knife in his back and take his roll. Then we can head for San Antonio. Ain't no telling what this feller is up to. We might get ourselves hung," one said.

"Looper, we will see what he has in mind. It will have to pay better than rustling the calves off the Hooker spread. What can get you hung quicker than rustling another feller's beef? Be quiet! I hear him coming," the one named Morris said.

Peal had snuck into the back of the barn while the three were discussing their newfound wealth. The nice Palomino gelding that Foster Peal rode plodded along until he stopped at the corner of the barn and started munching on a hay bale. The fancy dresser was not in the saddle. The three stepped out of the barn and stood looking at the fine animal. A few minutes later Peal and Holt stepped from the barn with their guns ready for use.

No one heard the two men that stood behind them until Foster Peal said, "Which of you is named Looper?"

The three jumped and turned to see the two ready to draw down on them. "Well! You kind of surprised us coming on us like that!" Morris exclaimed.

"I asked you a question. Do not make me repeat myself!" Peal demanded.

The man named Morris was suddenly aware that their conversation had been overheard. He pointed his finger at the smaller man to his left, and replied, "That be Looper. Why you ask?"

"So, you want to stick a knife in my back? You have a gun. Now is your chance to rob me. Pull it, or I will kill you where you stand," Peal said.

"Now mister, I was just funning. I was just making talk," Looper said.

"I bought you the clothes you are wearing. Take them off!" Peal stated.

257

Quickly Looper took off the new jeans and shirt. Now strap that gun back on," Peal said.

"Draw that gun, or I will kill you. You have to the count of three," Peal said.

Blackie had seen Foster Peal draw and knew he was fast and fully intended to kill this man. Before he could say anything, Peal drew and in the next instant the small man fell dead. "Well, I forgot to count," he said. Instantly, his pistol was pointed at the head of the one named Morris. "Now, you and you, take this man to the well behind this barn. It is deep, and you can drop your friend Looper in. My friend here will see to it you do it right," Foster Peal said.

Every night on this end of town there was gunfire, so no one even turned to look in the direction the shot came from. At one time the deep well had serviced the blacksmith that used this barn. Peal walked to the back of the barn and dropped the spent cartridge down the deep well. "Either one of you want to try your luck? You have seen me draw. Do you think you can beat me?" Peal asked

Morris was still looking down the well. "Mister, you made your point. There won't be any more need to shoot my friends," he responded.

"Morris, you need to get yourself a better class of friends. Do you know anyone else that will fill these clothes?" Peal asked mockingly.

"These-un's were the only two that I trusted," Morris said.

"Then you two will have to do. It's a small job that will not take you long, and I will pay you well. You two will follow this man," Foster said indicating Blackie.

Blackie instantly had a look of disapproval. He had had enough of Foster Peal's schemes. It never seemed to benefit him. Foster kept all the money and gave Blackie enough to take a bath and meals. He was tired of this game and wanted to go back to Louisiana. Messing with that girl would get his neck stretched. These two didn't have much 'telligence'. It was time for him to cut and run. He had kin in the bayou country, and he stood tall among the Breaux Clan. He would keep his poke packed and ready to ride away. For now, he would watch for an opening and at the first opportunity, he would ride for New Orleans. Being back home with Cletus, Lucas, and Leon fishing and boiling crabs brought a smile to his face. Now that was living.

The following day on a very overcast and foggy morning Tin Sloan, Jonathan Masters, and Cal Lacy rode out of Austin. Today the political elite would meet privately with Don Jo Verde. The sudden interest in Black Hawk around Austin had increased. Someone was stirring up the issue in all the saloons. The need to get this settled once and for all had become paramount. At the same time, the two Comanche braves left a place along the road where they had been keeping a watch for the well-dressed man riding a gold palomino gelding. Earlier on the same morning, they had watched as the black-bearded man had led two men away from the cattle pens along the railroad tracks. Making a mental note of this they turned for the tent city where Black Hawk was staying. It would be noon by the time they reached the settlement because of the wide berth they had to give Austin.

The three met with Don Jo Verde long before traveling to the appointed meeting place. Scratching his bald head Don Jo Verde looked at Pablo and Cal. "Tin, would it not be prudent if we sent Cal and the Professor back to inform the statesmen that we would be arriving much earlier than expected due to the increased tension over this issue? I would like Professor Masters to stay with Cal until this mess is settled and we are all safely out of Austin," Jo said.

"Good thinking! Cal, if you hurry you two can be having breakfast with your mother before the political wing of Austin wakes up," Tin said.

αααααα

Not far from the cattle pens Blackie Holt pulled his horse up and the three dismounted. "You two fellers have been told what you are to do. Just follow this railroad track, and you will run into the fancy rail car where the girl will be. Ain't nobody there but her and an old woman. You are not to hurt the old woman. Tie her up and bring the girl to the place where you were instructed," Blackie directed.

Moving over to an old barn, Blackie led a paint mare out of the barn. The horse was saddled, and a heavy pack of provisions was tied behind the saddle. "This is the horse for the girl," Blackie said.

"Wait a minute, feller! Ain't you supposed to be coming along with us?" the man named Morris asked.

"I take my orders just like you do and it works out better for all of us when we do. Our boss is no one to mess with as you well know. He always takes care of his men, and you will be well paid. You might even get more work after this job," Blackie said.

"Well, all right. It won't be hard to take this girl and deliver her to the meeting place. We have camped there a couple of times. I just don't like changes in the middle of a job. It just doesn't set well with me. I still don't see why he had to go and shoot Looper. He was my friend," Morris said.

"Forget about Looper. He said the wrong thing and the boss heard him. Don't ever bring him up again. It could get you killed. Boss does things his way, and he always keeps things moving. Just think about what you must do. Like it or not, everything goes just as he has planned. You will see! All will be well. There is a hood to put over the girl's head in the saddle bag. Now you better get going if you don't want to make the boss mad," Blackie said.

As the two disappeared down the tracks, Blackie Holt turned his horse eastward. There was one thing he knew… those two would be paid off in lead. Knowing Peal, he was sure he intended to kill him along with the two he had just watched disappear down the tracks. There was more to this than he knew and it did not include him. Foster didn't like eyewitnesses. It would take a month to get to the swamp south of New Orleans, but he would be home. For the first two hours he held the gelding to a smooth trot eating up the miles and letting the stress of the past three years of working with Foster Peal melt away. He made one quick stop at the stream by a trading post where he had a pack mule waiting for him. Now he had provisions to last him on his journey back home.

C24 – Well-Planned Evil

Miles in the opposite direction Foster Peal flipped his gold watch open and cursed under his breath. Blackie was useless and getting worse every day. It was time to break this association, and Blackie knew too much. After the girl was secure in his hands, he would make sure the three were not able to identify him. Blackie would be bringing the pack mule and all the provisions ready for a special trip Foster had planned for his twin sons and himself. Unfortunately, Tin Sloan changed all that.

Far down the coast of Mexico a remote Banana Plantation thrived in the tropical sun. The villa was a beautiful southern design visible along the stretch of wind-swept beach that ebbed back and forth among the coconut trees. What was not visible was the heavily armed men that secured the property from intruders. It had been a year earlier that Foster Peal and his boys robbed a train of a military payroll. The well-planned heist had not gone unnoticed, which led to an invitation to this tropical paradise. The owner of the plantation offered Foster Peal and his twin sons sanctuary and a business arrangement. After each well-planned job, Peal had only to make his way to the coast. There a boat owned by the man would always be ready to help Foster and his boys disappear. It was a perfect way of disappearing after each job.

It all started a year earlier when Peal had sat in a cantina on the Mexican side of the Rio Grande. A Spanish man had sat playing cards with Foster in a cantina The man seemed to intentionally lose a few hands before he started a conversation with Peal. Evidently, he had been sizing up Foster. Later that night over supper, the man indicated there was a man he knew that could use Mr. Peal's abilities and would pay handsomely. The man's business dealings in America sometimes required some rather harsh steps. Steps that Foster Peal was always ready to take. The plan was good. No one knew it but Foster, himself. He was to kidnap a girl and just disappear. Peal added to the plan that in due time, he would make a trip back to the Texas coast to kill the Black Hawk and the Rangers that had killed his twin sons. His plans were always thought out well and foolproof. He would leave no one alive that would leave a trail to him. *'Now where was Blackie and that pack mule? The other two with the girl should be showing up soon,'* Peal grumbled.

A few miles in the opposite direction Blackie turned on the main road and headed east. It was still early, and he had seen no one on the road. He hated to take this route. However, to get around a bad stretch of land fast, he had to take the long route. He feared Foster Peal would be after him if he had half the chance.

An hour earlier, the two misfits had taken the route in from town, hoping to overpower the girl outside of the railcar. As they approached the railcar, no one was in sight. They carefully looked into every window. The girl was nowhere to be seen. The old woman was napping in the chair. With orders not to hurt the woman, the two went back to the campsite.

Arriving at the campsite Peal looked questioningly at the two. "Where's the girl?" Peal hissed. "And where is the man that is supposed to be leading a pack mule?" Peal said not using Blackie's name.

"He met us with a pack mule and told us to get the girl and bring her to you. He said he would be along directly with the pack mule." Morris said.

"And the girl?" Peal demanded.

Morris responded quickly, "We did exactly as you said! She wasn't at the railcar. The old woman was asleep, so we came back here for more orders!"

Foster Peal stood with a cup of coffee in his hands. Suddenly his hands began to shake and he looked at the other two, and said, "You two stay here. The coffee is hot! Keep your fire low. I will return within an hour."

With that said Peal tightened the girth on the Palomino and rode straight east. Peal let the horse pick his own path as long as the Palomino was headed east. *'Lately, Blackie had talked of going back to Louisiana,'* he thought. Peal considered the very spot where Blackie would come out on the main road headed for the Louisiana border.

αααααα

Moving now on the main road Blackie felt a sigh of relief. The pack mule was not moving very fast, but Blackie Holt knew the country. Long before he had teamed up with Foster, he had lived in this area moving about stealing a calf here and there from the local ranchers. There was a cutoff headed north just a mile ahead. Once he was on that, he was home free. It was a rough country, but he would travel slowly. It would get him up high above the marshland before he turned back for New Orleans and home.

Just as he cleared the last group of boulders and settled the horse and his pack mule to a fast walk, a voice stopped him, "Hold up there!" the voice said.

Blackie Holt found himself facing Tin Sloan and the Black Hawk. They were headed for their meeting in town.

Tin looked Blackie over while pulling back his vest to reveal his badge. "My name is Tindal Sloan. I am a Texas Ranger. What is your name?" Tin asked.

"I am just a traveling man from Louisiana. I decided it was time for me to head home. I am not wanted for anything, so let me be on my way," Blackie replied.

Moving his horse to block Blackie's way Tin repeated, "I ask you what your name is! I have seen you around Austin a time or two."

"My name is Breaux from New Orleans. Now if you don't mind, I will be on my way," Blackie said.

"I know where I have seen you. You were in the company of a well-dressed man. What is that man's name?" Tindall insisted.

Suddenly Blackie lurched forward as his body was struck from behind by a rifle shot that exited his chest. His horse pitched forward and sent Tin's horse into a spin.

A second shot hit Don Jo Verde and knocked him off his horse. A third shot hit Tindal in the head, and suddenly there was complete quiet as two lay in the road and Tindall Sloan was laying back on his horse. Foster would have taken the time to ensure each of the bodies were dead with a second shot, but there was dust on the road. Someone was moving along at a good clip. He was sure that Blackie had not had time to divulge anything to the Ranger and Peal's marksmanship was the best. Turning his horse, he headed back to the meeting place. This little side trip set him back for too long a time. Now he would have to travel through rough country to avoid any people on the road. No one would know which direction he took, and the two he had hired for this job would soon be buried in a deep hole he had found while looking for the remote meeting place.

It was not long until Foster stood by the campfire eating a plate of beans and staring out across the hills. The two sat silently only glancing at each other now and then. "Hey boss, what happened to the feller what was supposed to be here with us?" Morris asked.

"I could not find him. I guess he decided he didn't want to work with me anymore," Peal lied.

"Hey boss, how about you paying us off! It will be dark in a few hours, and we be a-thinkin' we need to do some traveling. Maybe head up north," Morris said.

Reaching into his saddle bags, Foster took out three bags of coins. Handing each one of them a bag, he watched them empty the bag and look at the money they had in front of them. Just to gain their confidence he opened the third bag and started adding coins to each of the men's piles. "I guess you earned his share because he didn't show," Peal said with a smirk.

"That's mighty nice of you, boss. How much money you reckon this is, boss?" Morris asked.

"Too much," was all the answer that was given by Peal. Two shots rang out, and the two slumped over. Foster Peal gathered the money back up and put it back in his saddlebags. Before the sun had set, he rolled the last big rock over into the deep hole that would hold his crime until judgment day. Walking back into camp, he changed clothes to get out of the fancy ones he normally wore. He appeared now like the average pilgrim moving along the southern road headed for the coast.

Peal took time to file the hoofs of the two horses down. For the golden horse he rode, he removed the horseshoes and cleaned the hoofs. He was sure no one would be able to follow the horses to the barn. Just in case, he took all the preventative measures he could.

Earlier...in the middle of the road, Tin Sloan's horse bucked as Sloan slid from the back of his horse and lay crumpled in the middle of the road. A voice shouted! "Grab that big horse! He is about to run!"

A mule skinner tried for the reins but to no avail. Tin's horse bolted, and Jo Verde's horse raced with it back down the road headed for town.

"Louis, what we going to do with all these dead men? This feller is a Ranger," a teamster said, seeing Tin's badge.

Thirty minutes later the two horses thundered through town. There was blood on the saddle of Tin Sloan's horse. Cal

Lacy and Jonathan Masters had been sitting in a place where they could watch the road. Suddenly, Cal jumped up and shouted to several men crossing the road, "Sheriff! You men! Stop those horses!"

In an instant, they were headed back the way the horses had come. Quickly followed by the sheriff and a wagon he had the forethought would be needed. At the scene, Jonathan Masters said, "You teamsters take this dead man on to town in one of your wagons. There is nothing that can be done for him. Sheriff, we will take this wagon with Tin and Don Jo to the railroad car of Dr. Erlinda McAllen. She might be at the hotel with a doctor by the name of Dr. Lacy. Ride ahead and find them. Have them meet us at the railcar clinic of the Lady Doctor," Jonathan ordered.

It wasn't long until there was a large crowd of people around the railcar along with several Rangers that had heard the news. The news that one of the men was the Black Hawk started a storm of conversation. The missing daughter had not yet been discovered. "Maria, where is my daughter," Erlinda asked as she and Dr. Lacy made their way through the crowd.

"She left early to go to the hotel to find you. I told her she was to go straight to the hotel and not wander off," Maria, the maid said.

"Go to town and find her, Maria, and bring her back here," Erlinda said.

Several men carried the bodies of Tin and Don Jo into the railcar. Dr. Lacy and Dr. McAllen were already there preparing for their arrival. The sheriff and a Ranger stepped down from the rail car to a barrage of questions. Ignoring the questions, the Rangers mounted and headed back down the road to see what clues they could find. The sheriff dispersed the crowd and sent them back to town. Dr. Lacy did a quick examination of both men. "So, I finally meet the infamous Black Hawk. It appears his end will be as he has lived," Horace Lacy said.

"Horace, he still has a pulse! Are you going to try to help him? How about you, Erlinda?" Jonathan Masters questioned.

Erlinda had purposefully devoted her time to seeing what she could do for Tin Sloan. She heard the question but continued to address the wound on the side of the Ranger's head, saying, "This man has a severe concussion. His skull is fractured. All we can do here is make him as comfortable as possible. Just hope and pray he comes around."

"You didn't answer my question!" Jonathan exclaimed, removing his hat to expose all the damage that had been done years before.

"Dr. Lacy, you will have to find the bullet and repair the damage it has done.

We are on the edge of exploratory medical surgery. I will get everything ready for you. To answer your question, I do not treat Indians," Erlinda said.

"Erlinda, this man is not an Indian! He became one and adapted to their way of life. We just fought a civil war over whether this man should have the same freedoms you and I have or continue to be a slave. You hate what he did to you. I hate what he did to you. Now he even hates what he has done to you," Jonathan said.

"I know your pain, but God has forgiven him for all he has done. I had to do the same. Why don't you let God work out all the problems in your life? I can assure you it will work out okay. Wouldn't you say the same, Cal?" Jonathan asked.

"I will assist you, Doctor Lacy. If he dies, I don't want to wonder if I intentionally let it happen," Erlinda said.

A few minutes later, the maid entered breathing hard at the far end of the coach. "Señorita Erlinda, I cannot find Isabella anywhere! It is not like her to just not be where she said she would be!" the maid said.

"Cal, you and Jonathan go find Isabella and bring her to her mother. Do not come back without her. We have this under control," Dr. Lacy said.

"I will need several pieces of her clothing, so we can track her," Jonathan said.

"Surely you don't think something has happened to her?" Erlinda said in a state of alarm.

"No, I don't, but my Bloodhounds can find her quicker than Cal and I can," Jonathan Masters said.

Looking at the maid Erlinda said, "Give them whatever they need."

C25 – Where Do We Start?

Stepping down from the train car, Cal looked at Jonathan. "Where do we start in a situation like this?" he asked.

"Cal, you will now have the joy of watching Bloodhounds work. Isabella had to leave from here. Here is where we start. She had to walk to town. We will follow her scent until we find her. Bring me her clothes." Jonathan turned to the dogs and gave them a good sniff of Isabella's clothes. He commanded, "Hunt!"

The scent was strong, but to their amazement, it was in the opposite direction! The dogs kept barreling down the tracks, taking a sidestep occasionally towards small groups of flowers.

All four Bloodhounds circled the entire area. There was nothing found for two miles until far from the tracks, they all began to howl. The trail led through a group of trees that opened to an empty field overladen with flowers. There was Isabella bent over picking flowers. In her left hand was a bouquet.

Cal sat stunned in his saddle. "Professor, without your dogs, we would never have found Isabella this quickly. I am amazed and shocked! Isabella is safe. I know Dr. Erlinda will be happy and relieved that no harm has come to her daughter," he said.

Jonathan and Cal called out to Isabella. Startled, she turned around and saw Cal, whom she mistook for the Black Hawk. She turned and ran. Jonathan told Cal to stay back and rode his mule in the direction that Isabella had run. He found her crouched behind a boulder with the bouquet of flowers clutched in her hands. After some lengthy explaining that Cal was the son of Black Hawk but was raised by his White mother, Isabella agreed to go back to where Cal waited for them.

Cal gently spoke to Isabella and said, "Hi, I am Calvin Ben Lacy. Half-breed son of Samantha Lacy and the Black Hawk. I have spoken to your mother, and she told me I could talk to you. Your mother thinks you need a big brother. How do you feel about that?" Cal asked with a smile.

Isabella grinned and narrowed her eyes. "Mother sent the Texas Rangers to find me? A big brother? Are you a Ranger too? I love those dogs!" she said all in one breath.

"Little sister, you ask too many questions! Climb up here behind me and let's go see your mother!" Cal stated.

Upon arrival at the railcar, Isabella was shocked to find out that Black Hawk was being cared for by her mother! Isabella stormed into the surgery suite and faced her mother, saying, "You have the power to kill this savage! Why is he still alive? Hasn't he brought enough pain to us?"

Erlinda was distressed at the depth of hatred her daughter was exhibiting. She stepped back from Black Hawk and took a deep breath. She looked at Isabella and then back at Black Hawk, and said, "Isabella, I took an oath to help mankind. This very day, I have had to look into my very being and ask myself that very same question. The Black Hawk has changed not only in his ways but in his heart. He has asked my forgiveness for all the tragedy he has caused you and me. I told him I could not forgive him. Now, as he lies here on this table, his God touched my heart and softened it. I can see the change from a savage beast to an intelligent, caring man. His life change has changed mine as well. That could only happen through a Being more powerful than I."

Without looking up from his work, Dr. Lacy said, "Young lady, God promises each of us a new name when we get to heaven. Maybe he has decided the Black Hawk needs a new name now to help you give up your hate for him. Never use that name again. He is Jo Verde to you. It may be in God's design that you might call him Father."

Isabella, with her mouth opened and her eyes filled with tears, dropped the bouquet of flowers and ran to the door only to be blocked by Cal. Her hands flew up in a fit of rage and slapped Cal in his face. Cal grabbed her hands and held them until the anger subsided.

Cal looked into Isabella's eyes and said, "I have always wanted a spirited sister!" His smile was disarming and Isabella ran into the arms of her mother and wept. Once Isabella had calmed down, Dr. Lacy stated that they needed to get back to helping the man on the table. With that, the two doctors turned back to their work of trying to save the lives of Tin Sloan and Jo Verde.

Just the fact that Horace had made that statement assured Jonathan that forgiveness was a contagious act. *After all, forgiveness is an action word!* Jonathan thought.

In Austin, the sheriff laid his ink pen down and listened to the fast-moving steps coming down the boardwalk. The steps stopped at his office door, and suddenly Olive Shingle walked in. Walking over to the sheriff she leaned over and quietly said, "Sheriff, unless you can get the calvary here in an hour you better listen to everything I have to say. Your office has ears. Everything that is said in this office is quickly repeated in the saloons of Austin. Turn that bunch of drunks out of jail and let's talk," Olive said.

Laying his pin aside he considered the serious look on Olive's face. He knew she heard the gossip in the saloons. Saloon girls were a major source of information for him. Turning to his deputy, the sheriff said, "Albert, release every person we have back there and get them out of the office pronto. Tell them they can come back on Friday and get their guns." the sheriff said.

Moments later; "All right, we are alone. What is on your mind, Olive?" the sheriff asked.

"Sheriff, someone has stirred up the men in every saloon in Austin. Tonight, after midnight, there is a plan to take the wounded Mexican feller and hang him from the nearest tree. Every good person on the street turned tail and went home. All the bad elements are going from saloon to saloon and talking up a hanging. You won't find a handful of men that will stand with you against what you will be facing tonight. I don't know what you are going to do, but you better get a plan together and fast. My bags are packed and I intend to be gone as soon as I leave your office. Tin Sloan is near death, and until I see that he is all right, I will be on that coach he is in. If it was me when the train leaves Austin at eight, I would make sure it had that Dr. Lady's coach hooked to it."

Thinking, the sheriff turned to his deputy, and stated, "Albert, I want you to saddle up and head for the fort. Tell the commanding officer everything you just heard. Tell him I will need backup and quick. A crowd like this forming can burn a town down. No telling what they will do when they find I have removed the coach with Bald Jo Kline."

"Sheriff, the fort is a ten-mile ride. It will take me until midnight to get there," Albert said.

"Well then, you and I can stand in the middle of the street and face that bunch alone, or you can ride out. I will tell them the cavalry is coming," the sheriff said.

A few minutes later the deputy left in a fast lope.

The sheriff left the office of the railroad dispatcher and then made his way to the medical coach on the siding. Stepping up on the platform, he eased the coach door open and stood looking at Erlinda and Horace. "Doctors, someone has ignited the fuse of hate in every saloon in Austin. They intend to hang your patient tonight. Every saloon is full of thugs and the like. They are getting all liquored up. I have no time to get a detachment of cavalry in here to protect the Indian. So I made an alternate plan. A few minutes later, the coach lurched as the coupling was made. As quickly as possible it was pulled out to the main line. That night the train left early. Fortunately, the railroad was far from the closest saloon, and no one noticed the fine coach that was moving among a string of railroad cars.

Olive Shingle stepped to the far end of the coach and set her bag down. "Dr. Lady…Tindall Sloan is a friend of mine. I will sit by his side until I see if he will live or die, then the first town we stop in, I will get off. Is there anything I can do for him, or you, while I am here?" Olive asked.

C26 - A Disappearing Act

Foster Peal rode along in silence. He knew that no one in Austin besides Blackie and James Polk knew who he was. Blackie was dead, and no one knew his real name. Polk had left like the hounds of hell were after him when he saw Tin examining his horse tracks in the road. He could assume that Tindall Sloan and the Black Hawk would not be on his back trail. No one knew of his plan to kidnap the girl. She would never know how fortunate she was. His only concern was the tall man on the mule surrounded by his well-bred Bloodhounds.

Days later, the mast of a ship stood still in the distance. *'That must be the boat waiting for him.'* he thought. A sprinkle of rain fell and lightning lit up the sky out across the Gulf. Below him, he saw a fishing boat moored beside a long pier. It was a remote lonely place and an odd place for a boat that large to be anchored. It wasn't long until the overcast rain clouds and the late hour brought on an early dark. From his saddlebag, he took a lantern and waved it back and forth. A signal of the same came from the boat and he made his way down to the pier. It took only a short time to load the horse. Peal smiled to himself. He wished his boys had been here to see how their pa was always on top of his game. In a few days he would meet his new boss and a new and better life of crime would be his calling card.

Reaching the gangplank, Peal was met by a tall Black man dressed in strange apparel. "Are you Mr. Peal?" The tall Black man asked in broken English as he looked past Peal obviously looking for the girl he was supposed to have with him.

"I am Peal. The job will have to be rescheduled at a later date," Peal told the tall Black man with the gold earring.

Later that night Foster Peal lay in a warm bed that swayed to the small waves that were lapping against the ship as it skipped across the dark water. He smiled to himself as heavy rains blanketed the coast washing away any trace of horse tracks. Now he would revert to the well-dressed gentleman. The coast had been washed clean of his passing.

C27 – The Piece That Brings Peace

The schooner had been moored in a remote cove for over an hour as the sun began to rise on the fourth day. A pleasant village spread out along the beach on the east side of Mexico. The three Black men with earrings quickly secured the craft. Taking up spears and shields, the men waited on the wharf until Foster Peal disembarked. It wasn't long until a fine black carriage pulled by a team of black horses pulled up to the dock. The coachman was a slender Black man with the same earring as the three on the boat. Speaking to the man named Shaka, they conversed in the strange dialect. Then Shaka turned to Foster Peal.

"Mr. Peal, the master is waiting for your arrival. This carriage is for you. I will unload the horse and be along. These men will run beside the carriage and escort you to the plantation." Once he was inside the curtains were drawn, and he was in darkness as the coach moved along a path into the jungle. Peal did not like this feeling of being in a box, blocked from the warmth and brightness of day. *'I best make the story believable! I certainly do not want to be a slave here!'* he thought. As the coach drew away, Shaka stood and mumbled to himself in the strange language. Once they were clear of the small village, Peal opened the curtain to disclose the vast jungle they were moving through. *'One could never escape from this place!'* Peal mumbled.

αααααααα

Meanwhile, on a fast-moving train, Horace Lacy looked at the patient he had sat by all night long. What a turn of events. The very person who had ruined his life lay before him. There had not been any signs of progress for him or the Ranger lying on the bunk next to him. Horace had prayed for the Ranger but could not bring himself to pray for the Indian who remained motionless since the surgery. Standing, he touched the forehead of Don Jo Verde. A weak voice came to him from the darkness. "Dr. Lacy, for their benefit, tell the lady doctor I did not kill her grandfather, nor did I kill Professor Masters' wife. That does not excuse me for my part in the attacks. I accept that," Jo's voice trailed off. Dr. Lacy had no reply.

Olive Shingle looked at Dr. Lacy as he studied the two men lying before him. "I think he will make it," she said as she dipped a rag in a pan of cold water and placed it over the forehead and eyes of Tin Sloan. The cold compress made Tin move just a little, and Olive smiled. She had hoped for some response. Tin had not moved or indicated he would. This response was the first in the hours she had sat and bathed his face. A conductor moved into the room and talked with Erlinda. They would put her coach on a siding in a small town in the hills.

Walking to the back landing, Horace and Jonathan joined Erlinda and watched the train pull away from the coach. "Dr. Lacy, I have something going on in my life and I need your wisdom to understand what is happening. I believe it has eternal significance but am not sure how to address it," she said.

"Jonathan and Calvin are the ones you need to talk to, Erlinda." Horace paused and said looking from Erlinda to Jonathan, "It seems that God has provided you with someone to talk to! Jonathan, your insight into everything miraculous with all things eternal is needed."

Jonathan responded, "I will answer all I can with God's guidance. Now, Dr. Erlinda, what is on your mind, or should I say, what is on your heart?"

Erlinda looked at the two men and asked, "Jonathan, why am I feeling a change of heart towards this man (looking at Don Jo Verde)? He destroyed my future. Brought into the world a child that has been neglected and shunned by society! He has maimed and killed countless others. Yet, I see the change that God has brought to him that has turned his life around. This man has changed a whole generation of

285

people in Paso Verde! They have pride, skills, and such talent that only he could have brought about! Why did God choose such an evil person to forgive? Should he not be in the depths of hell that you so eloquently speak about? Are we not to fear this place and do our best through good works not to go to it?"

Erlinda continued, "I look at him now in such a weak and helpless state and I cannot feel the hatred I once had for him! I cannot wish him dead or even in anguish. He is so kind to me and to Isabella. Don Jo Verde seems to be repentant of all the evil he has thrust on me. His son even has forgiven him! I am so confused and terrified of this feeling. I have hidden my anger and hatred for this man for 13 years, and now—my heart hurts for the people of Paso Verde—and for me. What is it about God that has made this change—this miracle—I need to know! Please help me understand. What can I do to resolve this in my mind and heart?" she asked.

Jonathan took her hands and asked her to sit down. "Dr. Erlinda, we cannot always explain the miracles that God has brought to us. We can only thank him for His provision. Just knowing that your heart has changed means that you have opened your heart to the awesome power of God's forgiveness. Don Jo Verde was introduced to that forgiveness by a Bible that was given to him by a blacksmith. That blacksmith saw great possibilities in that man. With just the idea that he was to relearn the English language by reading it, he inadvertently learned not only the language but the magnificent words of life. He learned how to not only see the good in others but to see the good in himself. He was not always the savage that you first knew. Jo was a little boy snatched from his homeland to become a slave of society. His predicament was not of his doing. He had a strong body and a strong will to survive. If that meant taking up new cultures on the way, so be it. The power that consumed him to become a savage also helped him realize that he could no longer hurt those who were around him. He came to know that his power was in his kindness and humility. Jo asks for your forgiveness, not to make you weak but to make you strong. Anger and hatred can only continue to tear you down. Your daughter has assimilated that same hatred. She needs a mother who not only has forgiven her attacker but has asked forgiveness for herself. God is the only one who can do that. His love and forgiveness are the most needed in your life at this time. Perhaps then, you can forgive Jo for the pain he has caused you and Isabella."

"Jonathan, I want that forgiveness from God. I do not want to feel this hatred and anger toward Jo or anyone else. Please tell me how to ask God's forgiveness," Erlinda said.

"Well, Erlinda, if you believe that Jesus is the Son of God. That he was born of a virgin. That he died on a cruel cross and was resurrected three days later, I believe that your decision has already been made!" Jonathan responded.

Erlinda looked up into that jagged face of Jonathan's and smiled, saying, "I was brought up to believe that. When I was alone and lost after the attack, it became hard for me to believe that God existed. Yes, Jonathan. I believe all that! It has just been buried in the depth of my heart and mind. I ask God to forgive me, and I know he has!"

Jonathan genuinely smiled for the first time since Elizabeth's death. He shouted, "Glory be to God!"

Tin Sloan moaned and, to the shock of everyone around, asked, "What's all the shouting about? I have a terrific headache! Think you can keep the noise down?"

With that, Dr. Erlinda, Jonathan, Dr. Lacy, and Olive Shingles all turned and laughed as they ran to Tin's side. Olive looked at Tin, and their eyes met briefly. She turned and left the railcar. She was keeping her promise that when Tin woke up, she would leave.

When the commotion settled down, the doctors went back to attending Don Jo Verde. This time it was with a sense of urgency to help him recover. Dr. Lacy watched as Dr. Erlinda's demeanor changed towards Jo Verde.

'God has truly made a change in her!' Horace Lacy thought. He had not felt that depth of joy for a very long time!

A Cowboy's Prayer in a Broken World
By James E. Ferrell

Lo through a canopy of stars I gaze
My lonely heart to offer praise.
Across this vast and starlit night
A fiery streak of light goes by.

From far across God's endless reaches
Its journey's end—its bits and pieces.
Are gathered by the Master's hand
To piece together in His plan.

Above my bed, a moonlit night
Bathes my somber face in light.
Oh, for feathered wings of grace
To span this universe of space.

On Eagles wings, my soul would soar
High above this earthen floor
Seeking for that heavenly place
Forever awash in God's sweet grace.

Then came this night, a gentle wind
That stilled my anxious heart again.
For me, another day is done,
Another race I have run.

I've walked each step in God's sweet grace
And see above His wonderful face.
His plan always calms my soul
Since the Master made me whole.
Amen.

Made in the USA
Middletown, DE
28 September 2023